The Merchant

A Story Only Told to a Few...

UK Edition

The Merchant

A Story Only Told to a Few...

UK Edition

ISBN 978-1-3999-3622-4

Cover Design & book Formatting: UKinkers

www.sherifelhotabiy.com

www.ukinkers.com

The Merchant

A Story Only Told to a Few...

UK Edition

Sherif El Hotabiy

About the Author

Born in 1978 in London –the UK, then moved to Cairo, Egypt, in the early 1980s.

He started writing poetry in school, and during college, he won first prize in the English poetry contest for three consecutive years.

Also, during college, he became co-head of the poetry club in Egypt's best-selling English magazine.

After graduating in computer & management sciences, he joined Nile TV international as an editor, then moved up to be an editor-in-chief, reporter and news anchor.

He later used his creative and writing skills in public relations, advertisement, marketing, and copyrighting.

After spending six years writing his first novel, he sent the manuscript to Her Majesty the Queen to reward himself morally.

After successfully publishing his novel in Egypt, he founded UKinkers.com to publish 'The Merchant' in the UK.

Dedication

To

Dame Dominique
Natalie - counting stars together
Dr. Hala Banna
Dr. Youssreya Abou-Hadid

&

My Mother

Join UK inkers

We aim to gather all the people required for a successful publisher in one meeting point. Of course, we start with the writers and connect them with publishers, editors, agents, bookstores, book designers, filmmakers, PR & marketing experts, and even logistical and payment solution providers.

How does it work?

Authors send us their work. Then we feature authors we find offering an addition to the literary scene. Interested publishers and agents approach them, and authors contact editors, book designers or whomever they need to get their books to the scene.

And then, it all begins, and we add authors to the scene and enrich the literature further.

Whom are we starting with?

Extraordinary authors and whoever is ready to step out of the mainstream and join our community that works for the benefit of the Word, whether written in ink or pixels.

Why focus on the UK?

It is the capital of literature—the 'Hollywood' of books and the royal court of authors.

www.ukinkers.com

Intro

We are about to share the same feeling, so thank you for reading my book.

Sherif,

UKinkers.com

VI

<u>Prologue</u>

The Merchant

Every drop of every sea has touched one of my boats,
Travelling the world with my fleet,
Every sand of every shore has felt my boots,
Stomping the lands with my feet,
Eyes wide open and bold,
Careless to summer heat and winter cold,
Untouchable by no burglar nor pirate,
In the presence of mine,
Guns grow silent,
With every sunset and sunrise,
I bought and sold merchandise,
Until I saw that one beautiful woman,
For only she looks like one, I say she is human,
It is your heart,
That I want,
What price should I pay in gold, silver, or brass?
Words, vows or maybe love filled in a crystal glass,
I will not look for an answer,
Will not wait any longer,
I walked over the fire, water, mud, and ice,
And I know hearts have no price,
True, love is the worst thing at which a man would fail,
Attention sailors,
Pull up the anchors,
And set sail...set sail.

Chapter 1

"**O**ne step at a time," he thought to himself as he walked the seashore. His feet got heavier, and his head got lighter. He started walking the shore at the break of dawn. It is noon now. Yes, it is noon. Indeed, the scorching sun is right above his head. He looked at it, well, almost did, with nearly open eyes. He felt the sweat run down his forehead. It was time to rest for a while. He slid his backpack off his shoulder, walked a couple of steps into the sea, dropped to his knees, took off his sailor hat, soaked it in the salty sea waters, and then put it back on. He was trying to cool off. He splashed his face with some water and sighed, taking a deep look into the horizon, and thought, "Waves, just waves, one after another, just like steps, one after another. Where to? Where are my steps leading me? Somewhere...it must lead somewhere... or should I just keep walking pointlessly, just like those waves to the shore and back, and again, to the shore and back? Waves, minutes, days, years...steps...all to the shore and back. Is there any point out of all of this?"

Then it came into sight, just to his left, a lighthouse looming far away. He wore his backpack on his shoulder and sunk his ankles back in the sand as he started to walk again, but this time towards the lighthouse. He was drained, but he walked one step at a time...steadily...one step at a time.

After a long walk, he reached the lighthouse. He stood ashore and stared at it for a while; it looked like any other lighthouse he had seen before, but this one was old; it looked ancient, standing high at the end of a rocky land formation that stretched into the sea with waves crashing on its sides.

He picked his shoes out of his backpack, put them on, and then made his way to the lighthouse; It was a slightly refreshing walk as sea waves splashed on both sides, rhythmically, one wave after another, till he reached the door; He thought of knocking but the wooden door was all cracked up, and the doorknob looked well rusted, so it occurred to him it might be deserted. However, he gently opened the door, and a rather loud squeak announced his arrival just before he said, "Hello".

His eyes were struggling to spot the inside of the dark lighthouse. He had been walking in the sun for hours, after all. "Hello," he repeated in a louder voice, still no reply.

A moment later, he could see the stairwell of the lighthouse, rusty and silent.

Looking up the stairs, he thought, "Maybe there is someone up there; if not, it could be a place to rest for a while away from the sun." In cautious steps, he spiralled his way up the stairs.

The top of the lighthouse was round, a circular chamber of grey stone bricks and, of course, a wide glass window that circled the main lamp, a massive and powerful lamp that the lighthouse keeper switched on and rotated at night to guide sailing ships to shore. The sailor knew that. Though he had never been inside a lighthouse before, he expected it, and that was precisely what he saw as he made his way up to the light chamber, but he stood still as he saw a man sitting on a chair facing the sea. He wasn't exactly sitting; his head was tilted backwards, his legs were stretched, and his arms were hanging as if he had thrown his body on the chair.

The sailor stepped closer and closer. The man was wearing a thick grey wool jacket that just didn't fit the weather, navy blue trousers, black boots, a white t-shirt, and a dark grey hat that showed a little of his entirely white hair. The sailor instantly presumed that the old man was the lighthouse, Keeper.

"Hello," said the sailor, but the Keeper didn't answer back, didn't turn his head, and didn't move a bit.

So, the sailor slowly approached his right and saw his face

"I had never seen that many wrinkles on a man's face before," he thought. The Keeper's eyes were shut, and his mouth was open; he was obviously in a deep sleep.

The sailor stepped backwards quietly and was about to turn away. "Maybe I should just leave, carry on, or maybe..." before the sailor ended his inner dialogue, his backpack knocked an iron-cast teapot off the shelf behind him, banging it onto the floor. That was enough noise to wake the old Keeper out of his deep sleep.

"Huh...what? Who? ...who...you?" the old housekeeper

spoke in a panic.

"Easy," the sailor said, trying to calm the Keeper down, though he was intimidated by the old man's sudden panic. "Easy," the sailor repeated, but the Keeper suddenly tried to stand up, lost balance and fell to the floor. The sailor rushed to him and continued trying to calm him down.

"I am just a sailor...calm down, I am just a sailor."

The old Keeper rubbed the sleep off his eyes. "What are you doing here? What do you want?" he asked the sailor.

"I...I was walking the shore, just passing by...I needed to rest...I have been walking the shore for long now...very long," explained the sailor in a racing breath, trying to assure the old Keeper that he meant no harm.

The old Keeper stared at the young sailor's face; he seemed honest.

"What's your name?" the Keeper asked.

The sailor took a deep calming breath, exhaled as he sat on the floor and answered,

"I am a sailor...just a sailor, old mate".

Chapter 2

The water boiled inside the teapot. The Keeper stood in front of it, staring at the rolling water for seconds, then picked it up with a worn damp piece of grey cloth.

The sailor sat on a wooden chair a couple of feet away from the old man, silent, staring at the horizon. It is getting cloudy now, and the winds are picking up.

The old Keeper fixed two tin cups of tea, handed one to the sailor, and then sat on the chair opposite him, which wasn't too close or far.

"You are walking the shore, huh?"

"Yes, I am," answered the sailor.

"For how long now?" asked the Keeper.

"Long enough to reach this stranded shore," the sailor answered in sarcasm,

"You are a sailor then?" asked the Keeper as he pointed at the sailor's clothes and backpack.

"Aye," answered the sailor with a light smile.

The Keeper sipped his tea, and so the sailor did the same.

"That's good!" said the sailor right after his tea sip, "That is very good!" taking a good look at the tea, "What is this tea?"

"It is from the east...far from the east," replied the old Keeper.

"I have never tasted tea like it," the sailor remarked,

"How long have you lived here?" he asked the old Keeper.

"What?" The old keeper exclaimed.

"If I may ask, you must be living here, right? There is no village close enough to come back and forth to, so I figured you must be living here in this lighthouse, am I right?"

"You are right...yes, I live here. Been living here for quite a long time now...on this stranded shore...long enough that I have forgotten since when I have been living here," answered the old Keeper.

"I bet you are short on supplies; walking all this way, you must need food and fresh water," The Keeper added as he pointed to the sailor's backpack.

The sailor couldn't help admitting to the fact and answered, "Yes, I almost ran out".

The old Keeper rested his teacup on the table, got off his chair and walked to the sailor, who in turn picked his backpack up from the floor, pulled out a couple of almost empty water bottles and handed them to the old Keeper.

"You could have died of thirst," the old Keeper said as he opened the bottles, rattled a dull silver coin out of each, and then opened a small drawer filled with shiny silver coins. "Here, shiny new ones will keep your water fresh better than those rusted coins". He dropped one coin in each bottle and filled them with fresh water out of a giant wooden barrel.

"Where do you keep your water?" the sailor asked.

"Up there," answered the old Keeper as he pointed to the roof, "and when the clouds dry up, I borrow from ships passing by," he added as he filled the last bottle and sealed it back. He handed the bottles to the sailor, along with three sealed cans of food, some sea biscuits, and three more already filled water bottles.

"Thank you," said the sailor as he stuffed his bag with the bottles and the food cans.

"You are a well-mannered sailor," said the old Keeper, "but you have foolishly risked your life coming all the way here with just a couple of water bottles...so tell me, how did you get lost?"

"I am not lost, old mate; who said anything about me being lost?" said the sailor.

"No one has to say anything. You are a sailor who walks the shore, then you must be lost," said the Keeper.

"No. I am not," the sailor affirmed.

"So why are you off your ship, sailor? Why are you walking on the shore? Look at the world, son; it is land and sea; some farm the land, some sail the seas, but only the lost ones...walk the shore."

A brief moment of silence indicated that the sailor had too many thoughts running through his mind; The old Keeper noticed and said, "Seems like a long story...what is it? What is your story?" asked the old Keeper.

"I don't have a story," answered the sailor as he avoided eye contact with the old Keeper.

"No? That can't be. Everyone has a story...a story to keep...a story to tell or a story to live".

"Some lives are too simple to be a story," exclaimed the sailor,

"Life is too great to be simple," commented the old Keeper.

"Well, maybe mine is simple. But what about you? Do you have a story?" asked the sailor, trying to turn tables.

"You can't grow this old without having a story," replied the old Keeper.

"Well. What's your story then?" asked the sailor. As he glimpsed outside the window, the waves started to roll; he could hear them smashing into the rocks and spraying out.

"They say every lighthouse keeper receives one last visitor to hear his story," said the old Keeper.

"Oh! You think I am here to listen to your story?" the sailor seemed amused.

"Yes," answered the old Keeper in deep thought, looking to the sea.

The sailor broke the brief silence and said, "Well, it seems that I have to stay here for a while; looks like a storm is on its way..." he pointed out of the window to the now grey clouded sky, "so go on, tell me your story."

"My story? "

"Yes, your story!"

"My story isn't mine; my story isn't about me,"

"YOUR story is NOT about 'You'?" the sailor smiled, "What is it about then? I hope it is not about another sea monster."

The old Keeper turned to face the sailor,

"No! Not a sea monster...a sea Master."

Chapter 3

ALong time ago, somewhere in the sea, a ship sailed early in the morning. The ship's captain, wearing his full naval uniform, locked himself in his cabin, unrolled a map, pinned it on a wooded table and started studying it thoroughly. His cabin was exceptional. He had full crystal wear in his closet and a mini candle chandelier hanging in the middle of the wooden ceiling. The crystals whispered their clinks as the ship rocked its way through the waves. Though he gave firm orders not to be disturbed, someone knocked on his door.

"Pardon me, captain," a voice came from the outside. The captain recognised it right away; it was his first mate.

"What is it?" the captain shouted in annoyance.

"We need you on deck," answered the first mate.

"Is it an emergency?" the captain asked while leaning over his map.

The first mate answered reluctantly, "Not exactly... captain...but...."

"Then do not disturb me, as I commanded," the captain shouted firmly.

"Captain...it..." mumbled the first mate behind the door.

"In a while then," said the captain loudly, trying to refocus on his map, but the first mate abruptly said.

"Captain, I think we are being followed!"

The captain opened his cabin's door in a swift swing. "What exactly are you saying?" he exclaimed.

"That ship has been straight on our stern for a while now, captain," said the first mate.

"So?" the captain exclaimed. "They could be lost and following us for help. It happens, doesn't it?"

"In that case, we would have known who they are, captain," The first mate remarked.

"What do you mean?" asked the captain.

"They are hoisting no flags," said the first mate. Then added, "I am afraid they could be pirates, Captain,"

The captain hurried to the stern, wasn't hurrying out of worry but rather to get this whole thing over with as quickly as possible. Deep down inside, he didn't feel any threat. He opened his telescope and looked hard through it into the mist.

"That ship?"

"Aye, captain,"

"She seems pretty far from us," said the captain to the first mate. "They are no threat to us," he added as he folded his telescope.

"But they are not hoisting any flags," the first mate pointed.

The captain took a deep breath, exhaled, and turned to the first mate.

"I understand that this is the first time you sail under my command, and you are not quite acquainted with my methods yet. But answer me this, are they hoisting a pirates' flag?"

"No, captain," answered the first mate.

"Then, from now on, please do me the courtesy of not jumping to conclusions and following my orders strictly, one of which is when I asked not to be disturbed, understood?"

"Aye, captain," said the first mate in disappointment.

The captain headed back to his cabin as the first mate stood in worry.

The captain shut the door behind him as he returned to his cabin, nervous and mad that his time, he believed, was utterly wasted. "Pirates' ship!" he ridiculed.

He sat down and exhaled a deep breath to clear his mind and refocus on the map...his map...yes, he was known to be a mapping genius. He drew his maps that were to scale and accurate more than any other. That was what made him rank "Captain" in the first place.

"Where were we?" he mumbled as he set the crystal cups upside down on the papers' edge to keep them from curling.

The captain refined every edge, every line, and every corner of the map. He used all the tools available, marked every spot and even marked a calendar sail on the map, which shows the sailing lines best taken around the year seasons.

It took a while...an hour or so...of extreme focus; his head felt heavy, so he thought of taking a break, or maybe a nap, but his thoughts were interrupted again, this time not by a knock on the door, it wasn't a voice, it was a sound, a sound of a boom...then a splash. It sounded far away, but then there was a louder boom and a closer splash. His eyes popped in conclusion, for the sound of a boom and a splash could only mean one thing and one thing only...cannon balls. Someone was firing at his ship.

On deck, the captain rushed to the first mate at the helm, using all his strength to manoeuvre the ship into safety.

Sailors were rushing around, climbing up and down, opening all the masts for the ship to pick up speed. They were all trained and experienced, yet they were still panicking as the pirates' ship approached them faster and faster. Yes, it turned out that the ship following them was a pirates' ship.

"I don't get it," the sailor interrupted the old Keeper, "You said they were all panicking, right?"

"Yes," replied the old Keeper.

"It wasn't their first battle. I mean, all, or at least most of them, had been through battles before, they could be frightened, but panicking sounds a little too much, doesn't it?" the sailor remarked.

"Yes, almost all of them had seen battles before and fought well, but at those times, cannons were placed on the sides of the ship, mainly on the middle and lower decks. Guns were pushed through hatches that were only open to fire, and ships that shot first or had more docks to place more cannons won. Ships had to attack sideways and only sideways. This was how the battles they knew went. But this time, the attack was different. The pirates' ship had placed two cannons at the tip of the ship, and they were following the captain's ship; the pirates fired at them from behind, so the captain's ship couldn't retaliate. Their only chance was to outrun them, turn sideways and fire back at the pirates.

The pirates piled cannon balls in the middle of the main deck to balance the weight of the two heavy cannons placed at the bow of their ship or the bow.

They rolled one cannonball after the other to the bow to reload the cannons and fire.

"They are closing in," one of the sailors yelled in fear as he watched the pirates' ship narrow the gap.

The captain saw a fact in front of his eyes, what they were doing wasn't working; the manoeuvring was failing, slowing the ship down, and the pirates would board his ship sooner or later; he needed to run or hide. Instinctually he looked around for a getaway, and there it was, clouds of advection fog right above the waters; he instantly took the helm from the first mate and ordered him, "Get a dozen men to bring me a cannon from the lower deck and place it at the stern right now!"

The first mate hesitated. "Captain!"

"Now!" Shouted the Captain. The first mate rushed to carry out the order as the captain directed the ship to the fog, straight to the mist, without manoeuvring, hoping that the pirates might miss their target enough times. He needed to reach the fog. He sailed straight, windward to gain some speed, get deep enough into the mist to turn and fire back. The mast filled with air, and the ship's bow lifted as it gained momentum and headed straight into the fog.

In the lower deck, twelve cannons were lined up, six on each side, heavy guns of a black alloy metal, each resting on a two-wheeled wooden base and chained to the floor. One man was in charge of them all. He maintained them carefully and always readied them for battle. He couldn't skip that these cannons defended the lives of every person aboard the ship. Everyone trusted him with their lives and depended on his meticulous dedication, so he stood fast in his post, down in the shade. He rarely ever stood in broad sunlight. Because of this, his face stayed pale; that's why all the sailors called him "PaleFace".

"PaleFace," one of the dozen men called out, rushing down the stairs to the lower deck, or as they called it, the fire floor.

"We need a cannon on the main deck, captain's orders!"

"What? Now? How?" PaleFace exclaimed.

The cannon balls firing at the ship continued to echo, filling the air.

"The battle is on already; no time to explain; unchain the one closest to the stairs, hurry,"

After a moment of thought, PaleFace unchained the cannon and rattled it loose; he then nodded to the men who rushed to carry the heavy gun up the narrow stairs.

They struggled their way up as PaleFace stared at them and thought to himself, "That's either smart...or desperate."

"Did it work?" asked the sailor as the old Keeper paused to sip a little of his tea.

"The trick...the captain's idea...putting the cannon at the stern, did it work?" the sailor seemed a little more curious.

"No..." the old Keeper sighed his answer.

"The cannon was too heavy to handle; the men weren't trained for something like this, the ship was swinging, they were shaky, they dropped it off the stern...the bloody fools dropped a cannon into the waters in the middle of battle." The old Keeper paused, then continued. "As the ship reached the fog, the captain drifted the ship sideways to face the pirates with fire. They were stationed in the middle of the fog, and everyone hoped that the pirates didn't follow them into it, but soon they saw the shadow of the pirates' ship coming toward them. The pirates were persistent and skilled. The pirates angled their ship in a few seconds and hit first with double cannon lines on the starboard. They showered the captain's ship with fireballs, cracking wood and bones.

"Sounds like you were there! Were you there?" the sailor asked

"No," answered the old Keeper gazing outside of the window. "I wasn't...but a little boy was."

On the wooden floor of the main deck, a young boy curled his knees to his chest, covering both ears with his hands, and shutting his eyes in fear. He could still hear everything, though, the footsteps around him, the screams of the wounded and the silence of the dead. He heard wood shattering and cracking with every cannon ball fired. The sounds were loud, too loud to fade away, he wished it could stop, but the sounds, screams and booms, went on and on.

He wished, shutting his eyes harder and pressing on his ears firmer. The longer the battle went, the harder he wanted it to end. Until suddenly, it happened.

The battle sounds stopped. Slowly he opened his eyes and cautiously uncovered his ears. The cannons went silent, and a voice came from the high mast, shouting:

"It's the Merchant...It's the Merchant".

)))

Chapter 4

"It's the Merchant...The Merchant,"

The boy heard the man aloud over and over,
PaleFace jumped on the main deck, grabbed the little boy off the floor, lifted him with his arm around his waist, and hurried to the stern facing the horizon.

"Look, boy...look," PaleFace pointed the boy's attention away from all the blood and the dead.

It was hard to get a clear sea view in all the fog and cannon smoke. However, the Merchant's fleet was hard to miss no matter how thick the fog was. The boy glimpsed shadows, many shadows of small ships approaching very slowly. The pirates stood still; they didn't board or fire at the captain's ship; they stood still.

"They stopped the fight! The pirates are just watching us now," the boy said as he pointed to the pirates, who stood still steaming in anger. "How did this happen?"

"Because the Merchant is here, boy. In the Merchant's presence, guns grow silent. The Merchant doesn't take sides; he helps the ones in need, in any case. He will not attack the pirates but will not leave us to them. The Merchant will tow us to a safe harbour, and if the pirates try to stop him or dare to fire one cannonball at one of his ships, he will blow them away in a glimpse," PaleFace answered.

One of the Merchant's ships ripped through the fog and

smoke and gently bumped into the captain's ship. The ship had a small crew of five to seven men; the boy noticed as he gazed at the ship. Somehow all the crew looked alike to him. They were all wearing the same black trousers, black boots and white cotton jackets with a wide black belt tied around their waists to keep the no-button jackets closed. They seemed strong. Their shaved heads claimed them to be tough men, and their daring silent looks proved it.

"Are they brothers? All brothers?" the boy asked PaleFace.

"Sort of," PaleFace answered. "I bet you have never seen Asians before, boy...they are Asian men, boy...a far land...from where the sun rises,"

The small ships passed first. All ships looked the same, precisely the same.

The boy watched them passing one after another until they were engulfed by those small ships from all sides, filling the narrow gap between the captain's ship and the pirates.

The pirates stayed helplessly still while the Merchant's fleet passed through.

"The Merchant saved us, and look, the sun is out," he added as sun rays swept away the mist. The boy checked his palms back and forth and smiled. "Yeah, look, the sun is on my hands,"

"Is that him?" pointed the boy at one of the bigger-sized ships that followed the first smaller ones.

"Nope...that is not him...not in those," said PaleFace.

18

The boy waited a little while for ships to pass, and then he saw bigger vessels passing.

"Then he must be in these," the boy excitedly said.

"Young fella, those are for the sailors," PaleFace said.

"Then he must be in one of those. This must be his ship," said the boy pointing at a big ship sailing by.

"What are you thinking, boy? Would the Merchant stay in one of these? These ships are carrying his fleet's supplies. I told you it is the biggest fleet, and he...he has the biggest ship,"

"Bigger than this?"

"Yes,"

"Then how big is his ship?" asked the boy as he turned and looked PaleFace in the eyes, but before PaleFace could explain how big the Merchant's ship was, a shade swept slowly on the boy's face; he felt it, he looked at his hands and found the sunlight gone, now both standing in the shadow. PaleFace smiled and pointed upwards and answered the boy,

"It is that big,"

The boy looked upwards with wide eyes and an open jaw. He had never seen a ship that big, a ship that blocked the sun. Everyone was now standing in the shadow of his ship.

"That is Venus, young fella. The biggest ship in all the seas...this is the Merchant's ship."

Chapter 5

"The Merchant?" The sailor exclaimed.

"Yes, the Merchant,"

"Who was the Merchant?" the sailor asked the old Keeper.

"No one knew the Merchant's name, but everyone knew him; everyone knew that he owned the largest fleet on all seas, larger than any kingdom's navy at that time, armed stronger than any army, with long-range cannons, unbreakable swords with the sharpest blades, lots and lots of men and arms, and though he had that kind of power and though it was an age of raids where power served greed. He never attacked, never raided, and never violated. He was a man of principles who kept his promises and fulfilled his word. He could have taken any kingdom or raided any village; instead, he defended the weak and rescued the hit. And though at that time the seas were much more dangerous than they are nowadays, no pirate had ever dared to attack him; ever, no one could face the Merchant's fire force. So, he sailed safely through the world with that fleet and became the biggest trader in the world. He reached lands beyond anyone's reach, bringing things no one had seen before. He traded all kinds of goods to everyone, the poor, the rich and even the royal. He had a fortune of gold bigger than any man's greed, yet he was humble and kind at heart; he provided to the poor before offering to the rich. Yes, no one knew his name, no one knew where he came from or where he was born, and no one knew how he started his fleet and how it grew that big. His fleet was like a small floating village itself. A thousand ships! At that time, the biggest armadas were made up of 200, 300 or even 400 ships, but the Merchant had a thousand ships. It was the biggest fleet, and he owned the biggest ship of all, Venus.

"Venus?" the sailor exclaimed. "Venus, as the Greek symbol of beauty?" he asked the old Keeper.

"Yes,"

"Why was it named so? Was it beautiful?" he asked.

"It was made of dark reddish-brown wood, always polished like new, all ledges and edges were capped and decorated with real gold, its name was written in gold on both sides of the ship, and the figurehead at the bow was Venus herself, a complete heavy figurehead made of pure gold.

Venus looked beautiful as she glided over the waters. The ship was the most beautiful and the most powerful. It was three times higher than the highest ship, five times wider than the broadest ship, and ninety cannons strong. It wasn't just a ship. It was a wonder and the Merchant's home.

The Merchant built a house on its main deck, not a cabin, but a two-story high house. Because the Merchant loved the smell of freshly baked bread, they used to bake it in front of his house every morning.

"Bake? Did they bake fresh bread in ovens? On a ship?"

"They had everything, food, fresh water; some say they even grew their crops on some ships. They had cooks, tailors, wood carpenters and healers, everything one could ever need.

"It is hard to believe. I mean, I've never seen anything close to what you are saying, especially that house thing on Venus!" said the sailor.

"That's why Venus was the wonder of all ships. Sailors' stories were all about Venus, not just because of its beauty but also because it was rumoured that all his gains and earnings were stored in Venus' Belly throughout all the Merchant's expeditions. Its lower deck was said to have had more gold than the richest kingdom, and it all belonged to one man. The Merchant."

"Oh boy. The captain's ship must have felt very lucky to be rescued by the Merchant," said the sailor.

"Yes. They were lucky indeed," smiled the old Keeper.

Then the sailor asked, "So after he towed them, what happened next?"

"After the Merchant towed the captain's ship, some healers jumped onboard to treat the wounded in their special ways, using some kind of medicine from the Orient."

"Why aren't they wearing any earrings?" the boy asked PaleFace

Apart from the Merchant's crew outfit and looks, the young boy couldn't help noticing that all the Merchant's crew were not wearing any earrings.

At that time, all sailors wore gold or silver earrings, so

if they died or were helplessly ill, their mates could take off the earrings, sell it and pay for their journey back home.

"They don't wear earrings, kid," answered PaleFace.

"But why? How would they get home?" exclaimed the boy.

PaleFace looked at the Merchant's men in respect and admiration and answered the boy.

"They will never need to because to them...the sea is their home".

)))

Chapter 6

"**T**he seas were very different from nowadays," said the sailor

"And the lands, too," said the old Keeper.

"How?" asked the sailor.

And so, the old Keeper explained. He said that while the Merchant mastered the sea, Kings ruled the lands, and the strongest two kingdoms were the Red Marbled Kingdom and the Silver Kingdom, commonly known as the Silvers and the Reds.

The two kingdoms shared a border and a history. The Red Marbled Kingdom had a long line of monarchs, strong, victorious kings who invaded one neighbouring kingdom after another; and added one region after another to its vast lands. Their closest neighbouring kingdom was the Silver Kingdom, up a hill surrounded by sea waters from three sides and sharing a narrow land border downhill with the Red Marbled Kingdom the Silvers felt cornered, so they were the first ally and hand shaker with the Reds.

Together they invaded five of the seven regions that made up the world by then. Until one day, the Silver King died, and his son rose to the throne, and he was against the alliance, against invasion and war, against submission. So, the Silvers refused to join forces with the Reds for the first time. To save his pride, the Red King answered back by waging war against the Silvers to wipe them out, but the outcome was unexpected.

Geography had the final say. The hill had a narrow and rocky entrance and sharp, rough rocks. The Reds had a powerful and large cavalry but were not skilled enough to climb uphill and meet the Silvers' forces, so they were stationed downhill; Then, the Silvers foolishly rushed down to meet the Reds. Meanwhile, at sea, the Reds' warships sailed out of the Crab Gulf that the Red Kingdom overlooked. The gulf was enclosed by two mainland formations resembling crab's arms. On the east side, the hill stretched into the sea. And on the other side, on the west side, several isles, an archipelago, formed very close to the structure of crab claws.

Those isles were green, full of trees, and called the Tear Drop Isles.

The Silvers' navy waited for the red ships outside the Crab Gulf, who were instantly engulfed by the Silver ship line and defeated, wiped out, and sent to the seabed by the Silver armada, which consisted of 300 strong ships and hundreds of skilled sailors.

The Reds won on land but couldn't pursue and wipe out the Silvers uphill.

The Silvers won at sea, but their cannons couldn't reach the Red Marbled Castle and destroy it, so the two kingdoms stayed in an endless standoff...for years...neither one could attack, nor drawback, and the Merchant was a friend of both.

Chapter 7

A cannon boomed loudly and echoed from afar.

"What's that?" the boy looked for a comforting answer from PaleFace.

"Don't worry...look, it is the silver fleet...announcing the Merchant's arrival and welcoming him into their harbour, and they are firing their cannons in honour of the Merchant. No cannons are ever fired to attack the Merchant, only to honour and welcome him."

The Merchant was welcomed to every kingdom. His arrival was festive to everyone, especially the poor, who rushed to shore with smiles. To them, the Merchant's arrival meant salvation.

The Merchant's first day of arrival was called the "No Trade Day", where no trading was allowed. He dedicated the day to those who were in need. First, he gave away gold & silver coins to the poor, clothes to the needy and then spent the rest of the day treating and healing the weak and ill. His arrival to any kingdom celebrated kindness, an admiration of superiority and a fascination of a character, the Merchant.

PaleFace grabbed the young boy's hand as they blended into the festive crowd ashore.

A mysterious veiled man stood in the crowd; his eyes locked on the captain's ship; the Merchant rescued from the pirates. The veiled man was silent, unlike the cheering crowd.

It was a custom that the royal guards receive the Merchant at the castle's gate. They lined up on both sides in sharp discipline, one guard opposite the other.

After passing the silver sea gate, the Merchant anchored his fleet in the middle of the Crab Gulf, right in front of the Red Kingdom's castle, for no dockland was big enough to host the Merchant's fleet.

A small boat went to the ship fit to float over shallow waters, then ferried the Merchant to land, as a ceremonial guards' line up stretched from shore to the Red Castle's gate. He had to pass through the silver sea gate first to enter the Crab Gulf and then pass through the Red Kingdom to go uphill to the Silver Kingdom.

The Merchant stamped the shore with his foot; the guards announced his arrival by calling loudly and repeatedly, "The Merchant...it's the Merchant". Red Guards at the gate echoed back, as did the guards inside the castle. They all called out.

"It's the Merchant...The Merchant"

The Merchant walked through the hallways of the Red Castle. The whole floor inside was made of red marble.

Daylight beamed through tiny windows that barely had any view. The castle's front had so many windows, but many were decoy windows, fake windows that had been made to deceive the Silvers in case they attacked the castle with swift arrows or cannonballs. Because of this, no one could ever tell where the King's Hall was, the dining hall, or the Queen's chamber.

The old Keeper suddenly paused silently, deep in thought.

"I am listening," said the sailor, "Hello?" he said louder to grab the old Keeper's attention.

"Oh. What? Sorry...what was I saying?" the old Keeper seemed lost in thought.

"The decoy windows...of the Red Kingdom, the King's Hall, the Queen's Chamber!" The sailor reminded him.

"Oh! Yes. Of course," said the old Keeper, then paused.

"Are you all right?" asked the sailor.

"Me? Yes. Yes...I am," said the old Keeper.

"No! You don't seem all right to me? What's wrong?" the sailor asked.

"I...I just remembered...."

"What did you remember, old mate?"

"I remembered...She."

"She? Her...you mean you remembered her," said the sailor.

"No. She. The Queen. I remembered ...The Queen."

Chapter 8

A long time ago, kings & princes fought for land and wealth. They wanted more and more. They never stopped. It was an hour-by-hour battle in which the winner took it all. No King got enough wealth and power, land, castles, and armies. Amid all that greed, no king desired more than winning the Queen's heart. To be with the Queen was a dream, a desire, a challenge...she was beauty in human form.

"How beautiful was she? What did she look like?" asked the sailor.

"No," said the old Keeper. "It wasn't about how she looked but how she was." The old Keeper added, "Queen by birth, never been called by her name, always addressed as the Queen since she was a little girl, spoiled, obeyed. She didn't just move. She danced, barefoot, any place, any time, morning or night, they wiped the marble floors just for her, whenever she signalled music played, and she danced, oh did she dance. She moved to music better than a silk curtain to a summer breeze.

She wasn't the most beautiful...no, but she owned her beauty. She had the fairest snow-white skin. She bathed in cream and rose petals that her virgin servants picked for her every morning. She wasn't the most beautiful but had the longest, thickest, and straightest hair. Her servants combed her hair a thousand times every night. She wasn't the most beautiful, but she had the most expressive eyes that magnified her emotions in an unforgettable look to anyone.

On the night of her birth, all her family were murdered in a coup attempt; but the coup was failed by her guardian, a master guard of unmatched skills and strength. He looked after her as she grew up dancing barefoot in the halls of her royal palace.

Every King and prince raced to win her...but she could never be won...only the best of them got nothing more than her mere contempt. She wasn't the most beautiful... oh no...she wasn't.... but she was pride and glamour...she was...The Queen.

When she turned eighteen, her kingdom grew weak with political turmoil, hunger, and anger, and her army fell apart. It was a matter of time until a strong kingdom snatched them into slavery. The Queen then used her sharpest and most shiny weapon, her mind, and her beauty.

She announced that her hand would be given in marriage and spread the word to every royal court. Kings were crazy for the most desired Queen. She invited them all to the palace, to a Ceremonial Royale, a proposal, and a wedding at the same time. Kings arrived at the Queen's Ceremonial Royale from all over the world. They found the Queen in her wedding dress, sitting on her throne and waiting for her dream suitor. Her royal suitor, a prince, or a King. One by one, they all stepped in front of her and kissed her hand.

The one she accepted was to hold her hand and walk her through the hall. The rest would instantly be considered an invitee, a witness, an envious witness.

Of course, all the royal suitors brought wonderful presents to impress the Queen. She received a pile of presents higher than any of her kingdom's debts.

The valuable presents alone could have saved her whole kingdom, but she knew it wasn't enough. Power must be added to the equation.

She needed to stand in the shadow of a strong King, a King who is the King of kings...and so she picked him. With the might of her beauty, she had the chance to choose a king. Before anyone stepped foot into the hall of the Ceremonial Royale, she had already picked her king, the strongest and wealthiest king, The Red King.

Chapter 9
Ceremonial Royale

The Red King was the wealthiest, but he knew the competition was fierce, and wealth alone was not enough to impress the Queen.

Everyone at the Ceremonial Royale expected the Red King to walk through the reception with tons of gems and gold, for he was known for his royal wealth. However, the Red King walked down the aisle towards the Queen, who sat gracefully on her throne in her wedding dress, looking as beautiful as ever.

The Red King walked down the aisle with nothing. No treasure chests, tiaras, or exotic animals. No one spotted anything but his royal guards and himself. He knew he'd already grabbed the Queen's attention and stepped out of the competition. He approached the Queen with nothing but a smile, then pulled his hand out of his royal cape, and there it was, the Queen's gift in his hands. It was like nothing she had ever seen. It was like no one had ever seen. The Red King held a pair of crystal shoes decorated with diamonds, sparkling as brightly as the stars. The Queen was speechless, dazzled by their beauty.

The Red King bent his knee, kissed her hand, and slipped the Queen's feet into those marvellous crystal shoes. The Red King knew that the Queen would never be won by the most expensive gift, but rather by the 'one of a kind. He kissed her hand, took it in his, stood up and walked on his arm down the aisle. The envious had nothing but claps as they all witnessed the Red King marry The Queen.

The Queen was in her royal chamber when the voices of the guards echoed through the halls with the Merchant's arrival.

In her chamber, the Queen's maids always accompanied her, but outside her chamber, her guards followed. The royal guards she brought with her from her home kingdom.

Her guards' armour was golden and shiny. Her maids were all dressed in white silk, long-haired and fair, while the Queen was always dressed in one colour with a matching belt, collar, and hair ribbon.

The Queen's royal guards opened the doors, and she walked through, her silky dress drifting behind her. She always looked, almost floating, gliding on a breeze every time she walked. She walked barefoot, with elegant light steps...she walked to welcome the Merchant.

The Merchant entered the royal hall, the red hall, where the King sat on his throne.

"Greetings, your Highness," said the Merchant as he stood in front of the Red King.

"Welcome, my friend," said the Red King, "you are most welcomed to the Red Marble; it's been a long while," the Red King added.

"Yes, your Highness, we have stretched our sail beyond seas and rocks,"

"How far did you sail this time? You must tell me all about it," said the Red King with an amused smile.

"I have sailed far enough to bring you these, Your Grace," the Merchant said as his men promptly presented several chests. The Merchant always gave exotic gifts to kings and queens upon his arrival, things like silk, spices and even gems. The royals were always fascinated by the Merchant's offerings to them.

"More gifts? Every time you arrive?" exclaimed the Red King with a smile,

"Every time is the least I can do, your Highness," answered the Merchant.

At that moment, the Queen entered the hall.

"Good! Come my Queen, see our friend's surprising gift," said the Red King.

The Queen looked at the Merchant, glimpsed the chests, and then looked at the Merchant again.

"You are always most welcomed here," she said to him with a cold and rigid face.

The Merchant answered with a simple nod and a smile.

She walked to her chair and sat next to the Red King's throne.

The Merchant's gifts were extraordinary, exceptional pieces from every land. The Red King and the Queen were delighted, opening one chest after another until the last one, the iron chest with little holes.

The Merchant's men carried it and placed it right in front of the Red King and the Queen. Unlike all the previous chests, the Merchant's men didn't open it themselves. They placed it and stepped back from this one. The Merchant stepped in, laid his hand gently atop the iron box and said, "Your Highness, this is my special gift to you."

The King was eager to see the Merchant's unique gift to him. All the Merchant's gifts were special and exotic, but when the Merchant himself called a present 'special,' it must be something extraordinary.

The Merchant opened the iron chest. It was more of a cage, to be precise. Carefully, the Merchant dipped his arms elbows deep into the iron chest and slowly pulled out a newly born kind of animal.

"What is that?" exclaimed the Queen, "It is sleeping, isn't it? Looks like a newly born...bear maybe?" she added.

"No," said the Red King, "it is more of a wolf or a dog, its fur...or is that horsehair?" he added.

They couldn't tell and had to wait for the Merchant's answer.

"This is a rare animal, your Highness, the tribe that gave it to me, calls it in their native language, the Beast. The Merchant then pulled another one out of the iron box.

"I have brought you, twins of the Beast, your Highness," The Merchant added, "Their mother was killed by some ruthless hunters who killed it because of a belief that it produces a magical secretion through its fur as soon as it lays birth to its newly born. I tried to save the mother, but it was too late. In gratitude, the native tribe gave me the twins, and now I present them to Your Grace as a humble gift. Cage them behind walls, your Highness, feed them through iron bars until they grow strong, and when they do, nothing will protect your safety better than these beasts," said the Merchant.

The Red King and the Queen were stunned, and then the Red King broke the silence. "Your present is warmly accepted," then he ordered his guards, "Take them to the dungeons."

"Thank you, Merchant," said the Queen.

The Merchant nodded his head, "Your Grace."

)))

Chapter 10

Down the streets of the Red Kingdom, the Red King's Minister, still wearing a veil on his face, walked through the village at night until he reached the bar and entered. The bar was, as usual, regulars inside, chattering, laughing, eating, and drinking. The Minister wasn't there to fill his leisure with pleasure. He walked to the far end and sat on a small table, half hidden behind a pillar. In a surprising move, the bartender walked to him and slipped him a message.

"A Black Collar is here!"

A serious look grew on the Minister's face that sharply showed from behind his veil. Instantly, he stood up and followed the bartender to a black wooden door right behind the bar. He stepped down the stairway that was lit by dim candlelight until they reached the room below. It only had a table and some chairs where a man dressed in black was sitting, waiting for the Minister.

"It has been a while since you have been here in person," said the Minister as he removed his veil and sat in front of the Black Collar.

"Exactly," said the Black Collar, "Been a long while, and the Dean is wondering how much longer you need to take to find a solution to the problem? the Merchant, in case you need me to remind you," he mocked.

"Soon," answered the Minister uncomfortably.

"Soon! Do you want me to convey your idiotic answer to the Dean? 'Soon' is what you said long ago, and what have you done since? What have you even planned? The Black Collar said firmly; the Minister stayed silent; the Black Collar looked at him with a sarcastic smile, "You are nothing but one stupid bastard, aren't you? Minister!"

"Enough with your rudeness," shouted the Minister as he stood up and slammed the table with his hands.

"Enough with your ridiculousness," the Black Collar shouted, standing up in turn, "You are playing and wasting the family's time and resources. Do you think that you can play the Blacks?"

The Minister backed down and sat on his chair once again, throwing his body weight on it.

"It is a matter of time," panted the Minister,

The Black Collar walked round the table, leaned on the Minister, and said in a threatening tone, "No. It is not a matter of time. It's a matter of what matters, and the only thing that matters right now is the family's business, the Black family's trade that the Merchant is destroying. We are down to one-tenth of what it used to make, and the Dean is fed up," the Black Collar concluded, then picked his coat and turned to the Minister before he walked out of the door and said, "Find a solution or be one!"

"What is that supposed to mean?" asked the Minister, looking confused yet threatened, "You will know. But for now, no payments until you figure out a plan and take action." He climbed the stairs while the Minister sat still, puzzled, angry and afraid.

Chapter 11

The window slammed open as the winds stormed the seashore,

The old man stopped, stood up and closed it back tightly.

He used the interruption to stir the stew a little. It was half cooked,

"Well, that smells delicious," commented the sailor,

"When was that?" the sailor asked,

"When was what?" exclaimed the old Keeper,

"That! The story...when did all that happen?" the sailor elaborated,

"Does it matter?" said the old Keeper,

"Not really...I mean...yeah, maybe...because I can't believe that someone could get more powerful nowadays, I mean...like the Merchant, or even a couple of decades ago. The world is getting harder and harder. If I wanted to be like him, for instance, now...is impossible," the sailor said.

The old Keeper covered the pot, sat down on his chair, looked at the sailor in the eyes for a moment, took a deep breath, and then continued telling the story.

The Queen's maids lived in the castle, in one chamber for them all. Their movement around the court was rigorous. Their movement in and out of the castle was prohibited. Except for one. Her First maid.

The Red King had only one trusted minister since he

inherited the throne, expanded his kingdom, and built his empire. Though close to the Red King himself, the Minister had never asked the Red King for anything. The Red King admired that about him. He only asked for a favour when his only daughter turned into a beautiful young woman. The Minister then requested the King of Red to appoint her as the Queen's first maid. The Red King, of course, welcomed the Minister's request. And so, she became the Queen's first maid, the only one with the privilege of taking one day off every week. She slept over at her father's house, the Minister's simple and humble house. The Minister never wanted to live in the castle, though the Red King offered him to; the Minister insisted he stay in the same humble cottage that he lived in with his late wife, a way to cherish his memories, he justified to the Red King. It was another thing the Red King admired about his minister.

But that never made his daughter happy; a single sleepover in her father's house every week, very limited movement in and out and even around the Red Castle was frustrating for her. Being the Queen's first maid, or even just one of her maids, wasn't a full-time occupation. It was a life, a whole life, dedicated to the Queen's service. The first maid always wanted a life of her own; she wanted a life for herself.

The Red King and the Queen receiving the Merchant was one of the few opportunities the maids had to do whatever they felt like doing, resting, napping, giggling, reading or even taking a brief stroll through the Royal gardens. Every maid had something different to do. But not the first maid, she always did the same thing recently. She ran to the same place to see the same person, her only love, the Merchant's First Man.

"I have missed you," said the First Man as he hugged the first maid, or, as the Queen calls her, Prima.

"Longing for you is torturing. Missing you can't merely express the feeling that overwhelmed me when you left," Prima said, then pulled out of his hug to look at his face, "and the worst thing is I never know when you are coming back."

"I am back now, aren't I?" the First Man said to Prima as he caressed her face.

"Look what I've got you," he opened a small wooden box with a diamond ring inside it.

"This a diamond Prima. It is said to have been originally coal, but somehow, it turns into a diamond after being deeply embraced by mighty mountains. Your love Prima embraced my heart as such, and it turned every piece of black coal in my world into a sparkling diamond,"

Prima and the First Man stayed in each other's arms and spoke softly, whispering to one another at the far end of the royal gardens. The First Man knew how to sneak in and out through the bushes and trees and climb over the walls without being spotted by the castle's guards.

A bell rang; Prima turned sharply to where the sound came from. It came from the castle. "Oh no! That soon?" she said in frustration. The bell ringing was the Queen's call for her maids to be back. A crystal bell with a golden handle that she rang rapidly.

They stepped away from each other while still holding hands,

"When would I see you again?" she asked,

"After tomorrow, my love," the First Man answered.

The bell rang faster and faster, trying to catch up with the Queen's impatience.

"I have to run back to the castle," Prima said as they stretched their arms long enough to let go of each other's hands. The First Man stepped back into the bushes to climb the trees over the wall and saw Prima. "After tomorrow, my love. After Market Day." Then he disappeared into the bushes.

Chapter 12

After a long day of helping people, the Merchant returned to his ship to dress up for the Red King's dinner. He'd rather skip it but couldn't turn down the Red King's invitation.

Music played, and food of all colours and tastes was set on the long wooden table. Dancers swirled around. The Merchant finished his meal first. He didn't eat as much as the Red King. The Queen, however, barely ate anything.

"Huh," said the Red King, "Well, that is what I call a King size meal," as he banged the table with his fists. A servant refilled the Red King's cup right away.

The Red King grabbed his drink and stood up as he said, "Merchant, would you join me on the terrace? That fat turkey I ate pushed out all the air in my chest. I need a fresh breeze."

The Merchant stood up instantly, "Of course, your Highness".

They walked away from the table and to the terrace.

The Queen sat in silence while the music played.

The Red King and the Merchant entered the terrace. It was vast, overlooking the woods at the back of the castle.

"Huh air, fresh air, I love this terrace, too bad it is not facing the seaside. Only if it weren't for those bloody Silvers, I would have had my terrace overlooking the sea. I would have had any terrace in the world," said the Red King, who seemed a little tipsy.

"Make peace with them, and you won't have to hide your open spaces or narrow your windows," said the Merchant.

"What?" the Red King said and turned to the Merchant,

"Peace? With 'them'?" taunted the Red King, "They want no peace," he added, "I tried to make a deal with them a thousand times. Yet, none,"

"They didn't refuse peace; they refused war, your Highness; if your deal requires them helping you invade the rest of the world, then, yes, no peace," The Merchant said

"What are you asking me to do? Huh? You said it yourself, 'the rest of the world.' I am almost the King of the world. Look at these flags," the Red King pointed upwards, "Seven poles but only five flags, seven poles for the seven corners of the world. My grandfather put one flag up there. My father also put one flag up there, but I...I added three flags, three! They spent their lifetimes just to add one, and I added three corners of the world to the Red Kingdom, but I know that these three won't be as significant as adding five. I will then be the King of the world, not an 'almost' King of the world," said the Red King.

Their conversation was interrupted by a sudden change in music; the players played at a louder volume. The servants emptied the hall and moved out all the tables and chairs. The Queen stood barefoot on the red marble floor and started to dance.

The Red King gazed at her with passion and lust. The Merchant watched her. Everyone did. It was something to watch and never turn a back to, for no one had ever danced, as did the Queen.

She danced and danced, and as her dance neared its end, the Merchant asked the Red King's pardon and left the hall. The Queen ended her dance as she saw the Merchant leave. She paused, breathed deeply, and watched him walk out.

)))

Chapter 13

People in nearby villages rushed to the Red Kingdom's main marketplace. They flocked in the early morning, the rich, the moderate, the humble and even servants. Everyone ran to the Merchant's Market Day.

His men had to set up extra tents to stretch out the marketplace to display all the merchandise. There was something of interest for every item.

The Merchant never attended the market, but he supervised every piece of merchandise taken out of the ships and waited by the docks to check the unsold pieces back into storage.

He delegated all the market's trades to the First Man, which made it the busiest day for him, tiring, yet the First Man was always up to it, always reliable and trustworthy.

Clothes, spices, ornaments, crystals, gems, jewellery, exotic animals, and herbs all were for sale.

The veiled man from the bar walked around the market with slow steps and extended glimpses, observing every detail, the number of tents, and the market trades. The Merchant's guards whom he always sent to secure the market,

The veiled man was roaming around the marketplace, looking at everything, and just before the Merchant's guards noticed him, he jumped on his horse and rode away swiftly. He kept riding at a fast pace through the woods. He seemed to have known his way through the woods pretty well, riding swiftly from one route to another until he reached the Red Castle. He stopped his horse, took off his veil and cape, and put them in a bag hanging on the horse's side. Then he rode his horse towards the Red Castle much faster. He kept speeding as he got closer to the Red Castle and up to the castle's front gate. The guards saw him riding towards them with no intention of stopping and asking permission to enter. Yes, because he didn't have to.

"The Minister, it's the King's Minister; open the gate," they shouted atop the walls. Instantly, the gate guards opened and saluted the Minister as he passed by.

The Minister entered the throne hall. The royal guards saluted him. He walked from the entrance until he stood in front of the Red King.

"Your royal Highness," said the Minister as he bowed before the Red King.

"Haven't seen you since yesterday!" said the Red King, "You weren't even here for the Merchant's reception,"

"I'd rather watch your back. I was gathering intelligence, Sire," said the Minister.

"As usual," smiled the Red King.

"I am at your service, your Highness," the Minister said with pride.

"What did you find out this time?" asked the Red King.

"He saved another ship," answered the Minister.

"I don't know why this worries you so much," said the Red King.

The Minister tempered his nerves a little and answered after exhaling a deep breath.

"Sire, it means one thing, and it is the only thing concerned about the kingdom. It means his fleet is getting bigger and larger than any other, and no pirate can defeat him. No pirate can even dare to attack him. He is the strongest out there on the seas. The seas are our weakness. Your Highness, you see him as a friend, but I see him as a threat, especially because he is not just a friend of yours. He is friends with everyone, even the Silvers, our arch army, your Highness." The Minister lowered his head and kept his eyes on the ground as he finished his polite outburst.

The Red King took a deep breath and exhaled as he looked to the narrow windows of his hall that barely let a light beam in. At that moment, the Minister continued, "All that stands between you and the world is a strong fleet, and the Merchant has the biggest one. The Red crown could rule the world for a thousand years...only if you finally get the Merchant to join us, one day he might finally agree, but until that day comes...the Merchant, your friend...to me... is a threat, Sire."

The Red King remained silent, looking at the Minister standing before him.

"You may now go, go now, Minister,"

That wasn't exactly the answer the Minister was expecting to hear, but royal orders must be followed.

"Yes, Sire," the Minister nodded and walked out of the throne hall. The guards shut the door behind him.

Chapter 14

Luckily, Prima's day off followed Market Day. The First Man was free, so they spent the whole day together. A picnic date was their favourite, by a lake, in a hidden spot wrapped around by trees, plants and flowers. The light breeze, sun rays and birds singing gave the best touch to the scene. They loved being there; they loved being with each other.

"So, you have seen the whole world, haven't you?" said Prima with smiling admiration as she laid her head on the First Man's lap.

"Yes, I did," he answered while tenderly running his fingers through her hair. She sat in excitement, "Then tell me how it feels?" she asked, "How does it feel to step into a new town, to see new people, completely different cultures in too many ways...what is that like?"

"When you arrive in a town, a town you have never been to, you must feel it before you explore it. You must fill your senses with it. You see it with your eyes, you feel it with your hands by touching its walls and houses, you taste it by eating its food, and you hear it by listing to its music. You inhale it by taking a deep breath over its highest hill. Only then do you get to feel it," the First Man said.

"You make it sound like a person," she said.

"Well, towns are made of people. People are towns; I've always felt that women are like towns."

"So, I am a town," smiled Prima, "so how you get to feel me? I don't have streets or houses or music bands,"

"I see you by looking at every inch of you and every detail of your beauty. I go to your favourite places, listen to your favourite music, taste your favourite food, inhale the scents of your favourite flowers, and everything I see, touch, smell or taste makes me fall in love with you more and more, Prima."

"So, what would you call me if I were a town?"

"You?"

"Yes,"

"Home. You are home Prima; you are my home."

)))

Chapter 15

The Red King strolled the Royal Garden with the Queen.

Her maids and his guards followed a step behind. The Red King looked happy, and the Queen seemed preoccupied with deep thought, yet still, she appeared to listen to the Red King.

Suddenly the guards stomped their spears and announced

"The Merchant,"

The Red King and Queen stopped and turned to find the Merchant striding towards them.

"Your royal Highness, your Majesty, " he greeted the Red King and the Queen.

"Perfect timing," the Red King said, "We were just about to ride out," He pointed to the two horses in front of the Royal stables.

"Join us. I will have them pull an Arabian horse out of the stables in a blink!" said the Red King.

"Appreciate it, but no need, your Highness," answered the Merchant, "I came to bid you farewell. Tomorrow is 'No Land Day'. We'll all stay aboard the whole day and prepare for the next sail, no one is allowed to step on land, and I will be sailing out the day after."

"Oh yes," said the Red King as he mounted his horse lightly.

"No land day already? I thought you would be spending more days here. Well, see you next time. Try to come back soon," said the King as he noticed that the Queen hadn't mounted her horse yet, "Aren't you joining me, my Queen?"

"No," answered the Queen, "I will be heading back to my chamber, for my mind had skipped a matter at hand," she added.

"Very well," the Red King, who didn't expect the Queen's sudden change of mind and seemed uncomfortable for a second, but he quickly turned to the Merchant, "Are you sure you don't want to join me now, Merchant? There is a free horse right here," He pointed to the Queen's horse.

"No one is ever allowed to ride the King's or the Queen's horses", the Merchant thought and answered, "Thank you, Your Grace, but as a matter of fact, I don't ride horses."

"You don't ride?" the Red King exclaimed.

"Oh, no, I do, Your Grace! But not horses. I ride waves, only waves, your Highness,"

"Right," smiled the Red King, then said, "Well then, have a safe ride, Merchant". Then he took off on his horse, and the royal guards followed.

At that moment, just as the Red King and his guards reached the wooded tree line, the Queen turned sharply to the Merchant and said nervously.

"What are you doing?"

"I am not doing anything," answered the Merchant.

"Exactly," said the Queen as her eyes gazed at him, then added, "you are not doing anything; you are not answering my letters. You do not love me back,"

"I never read your letters to answer back," said the Merchant.

"Why are you doing this?" she blamed him.

"You shouldn't be writing me any letters. You are a married woman, and I will never stab any man in his back."

"Okay, just read them, read my letters. I want you to know how I feel," she pleaded.

"I know, and you should stop...you must stop," the Merchant said firmly.

"Stop!" The Queen raised her eyebrows, "You telling me to stop! I am not the one who should be stopping anything. You are the one who should stop," she poked his chest in anger.

"Me? Stop what?"

"Stop this". She waved around "all this, the fleet, the Merchant, master of the seas, a friend of kings and queens, the man who own Venus, the ship with a golden belly, stop all those stories about you, the admiration, and the wonder, stop this magical world of yours, where you have no equal, stop being this noble savage who is feared and loved at the same time. Stop being like no other, stop being the Merchant...then I will stop."

The Queen walked away, and her maids followed as the Merchant stood in the royal gardens and watched her leave.

Chapter 16

The Minister woke up early in the morning, put on his formal clothes and stepped downstairs, and to his surprise, found Prima sitting on the wooden table in the humble dining room.

"Prima!' shouldn't you be at the Red Castle by now, with the Queen?"

"I'll be a little late; it's all right. I've asked her permission," she said.

The Minister poured himself a cup of tea and sat at the head of the table. "Are you all right, darling?" He seemed concerned.

"Yes, father, don't worry...I...I just wanted to talk to you about...a matter." She stumbled and seemed reluctant to open the subject.

"What is it, sweetheart?" he asked. His tender tone encouraged her to speak up.

"Father, someone asked my hand in marriage."

"You never failed to surprise me, haven't you, Prima?"

"I love him, father," she said.

"Who is he? "

"The First Man."

"Who? Whose first man?"

"The First Man, father! The Merchant's First Man".

"I want to spare you my mockery, but no matter what title they gave him on that ship, it is worthless here in this kingdom. The first man of a ship is a first of none...he is just a sailor Prima...you want to marry a sailor?"

"A sailor is what he does... but it is not who he is," she defended.

"But that's what you will be, a sailor's wife, living on the fallen crumbs of what the rich bites. Waiting for him on land while he leaves and leaves and leaves every time without knowing when you will see him again. You will be poor and worried. That's what you are asking my permission for! You are the Royal Minister's daughter, my only daughter... the least you could marry is a wealthy noble man... perhaps a prince or even a King one day."

"But father..."

"No! my answer is No!" he interrupted her.

Prima leaned her head on the table and started crying.

Seeing her like this, the Minister took a deep breath and tried to comfort her.

"Prima. Your mother and I have done everything, and I mean everything, to give you a happy and wealthy life. It's all been planned, and we have committed to the plan. I am not giving up now after all this! After she's gone! I promised Prima, on her death bed, I would not break my promise."

"But you will be breaking my heart," she cried.

"I swore to secure you. Why do you think I've put you in the castle in the first place? You are the Minister's daughter and the Queen's first maid. If you are going to step out of the castle, you should be stepping into another. I would only marry you into a wealthy and honourable marriage. Not a sailor. See you in the castle... don't be late."

He left the house while Prima cried her heart out.

)))

Chapter 17

The Queen watched her maids fill her bathtub with creamy white water. Every night the Queen bathed in creamy waters. She had a bathing tub built in her chamber, carved in the marbled floor, squared by four wooden pillars that hung with delicate white curtains on all four sides. The curtains were thin and could be seen through and were partially closed. Still, it gave the Queen a sense of royal exclusivity, and she liked how the curtains moved with the slightest breeze.

After filling the tub, the maids stood around it and waited for the Queen. In deep thought, the Queen stood up and strolled across the chamber towards the tub. She handed her gown to one of the maids on the way, stepped lightly up the marble platform and then...and then, she stepped down into the creamy water, so smoothly step by step that she hardly even agitated the waters, like...a...like a Queen taking a bath. She dipped, sat there for a while, rested, eyes closed.

When she finished, she took the other steps out of the tub. She had steps in and out of the tub; she never liked to turn back; she always liked moving forward. As she stepped out of the tub, her maids instantly wrapped a purple silk robe around, then she, as usual, walked to her dresser, sat on the chair and then Prima combed her hair. Prima had to comb the Queen's long hair every night in a thousand slow strokes while the maids stood around in service. The Queen stayed silent in her deep thought. Prima was heavy at heart, but she carried on every night's same routine, the same beauty ritual.

That night after the Queen finished her beauty routine; she dismissed Prima and the rest of the maids. They left to sleep in a room adjacent to her Majesty's own. She dismissed them but didn't go to her bed as usual. She stood by the dresser, placed her hands around a candle lamp, picked it up slowly and walked to the narrow window next to her bed. She put the lamp on the edge of the window, looked at the shadows of the Merchant's ships in the bay and thought, "Fine! Don't read my letters, but when you look at the castle, you will see my candle lit all night, and I know that you will know it's me, you will know that I am sleepless, you will know that between love and anger I lay, restless, because of you."

The Queen wasn't the only one sleepless and restless that night.

Prima walked through the dark hallways in her nightgown. How could she sleep? The only one she has ever loved is about to sail off, and she doesn't know where or when he will return. She reached the castle's top floor.

The Red guards just let her be. They are used to seeing her wander the hallows at night, but she looks sad, gloomy, and distant that night. The breeze lifted her light rose-coloured nightgown as she walked past the red guards; it gently caressed their iron-shielded chests while she took the stairs to the roof.

She stood under the moonlight and looked at the sea where the Merchant's fleet floated. They were all on board, seemed all awake, the ship's lights sparkled over the waters, a thousand ships or more.

"I am sorry I had to tell you every harsh word my father told me. I am sorry I had to hurt your heart through the ears that have never heard anything from me but love. I am sorry I can't comfort you now. I don't even know where you are now. Where are you, my love? Which of those ships beholds you?" she whispered, "I want to be with you. We belong together." Her tears dropped down one after another.

Chapter 18

"What am I in?" one of the Queen's guards thought to himself as he made his way back to the castle. He had just delivered the Queen's sealed letter to the Merchant's fleet. He questioned it every time. "Why does it have to be me? She orders me every time; Sneak out, go unnoticed to the Teardrop Isles, swim quietly to the Merchant's fleet, hand them the letter and sneak back in. Why doesn't she want anyone to know about it? What is in that letter? In all those letters? What if I get caught? Does the Red King know about this? Maybe she is doing it for him... some secret arrangement he has with the Merchant!" Finding comfort in the thought, he indulged in it. "Well, that makes perfect sense, especially that the Silvers have their spies everywhere." Just as he was about to rest on the thought, he remembered that the Merchant returned many letters without even opening them. "So, what does that mean now?" he spun back to confusion. "This is too much for me to grasp and too threatening to linger around. I must ask, but whom? The Queen? Of course not. The Red King, the Minister, no, no, no. Someone from the Red Castle, some close to the Royals...Prima! I will tell Prima, and she will explain it to me. Or if she finds anything wrong with it, she will be the one to handle it. She will know what to do. She will. She must."

As he approached the last isle facing the Red Castle, he

stopped, looked around, ducked down as he walked slowly to the shore, and saw the red guards patrolling on the other side. "I have to go to Prima as soon as I can." He dipped in the waters quietly and swam back to the Red Castle.

Chapter 19

After months at sea, the Merchant's fleet finally reached land. A faraway land out of the reach of the Red King. The furthest land of all, the kingdom of World's Edge, one of the few kingdoms behind rivers and seas that the Red King couldn't invade. World's Edge was a humble Kingdom with the smallest castle, ruled by the oldest King. As soon as the ships neared land, the Merchant took a small boat himself to land. He was eager to reach the shore and didn't wait for the fleet to anchor.

The First Man knew the reason behind the Merchant's eagerness. Everyone knew. The Merchant jumped off the boat, splashing his steps towards the shore. He ran and ran; he wanted so eagerly to see her and only her; he ran to Isabella. Everyone knew her. Everyone knew her story.

Isabella's father was a gipsy, a traveller who met her mother one day in the woods near her camp. Her mother was from another clan, a Romanichal Traveler, Isabella's father, fell in love with her exotic beauty as soon as he laid his eyes on her. She felt for him, too. They decided to get married, but she was promised to one of her cousins. Nonetheless, her stubbornness was greater than her clan's fury, and she married the one she loved after leaving her clan and joining her husband's. She would have been happy, but they cursed her; yes, her clan cursed her by the wolves, three fierce wolves. She heard them howl every night, no matter where she travelled. She heard the howling night after night, week after week, month after month; the wolves howled and followed. They tried to ignore the threat and live happily in love, and they did for a while, but as she got pregnant, the howling got closer and louder, and fear grew and overshadowed their love and happiness. One moonless night she broke down, she was getting close to giving birth, and she feared for the lives of her beloved. She cried her tears out for hours. Angry to see her like that and fed up with the threat, Isabella's father took his axe and went out for the wolves. She couldn't stop him; no one could, everyone saw him storm into the dark woods, and they heard they heard him, they heard them, roars and screams till the sounds faded out. He never came back. They looked for him, they found one dead wolf he managed to kill with his axe, but they never found him.

Isabella was born a few days later. Grief drove everyone to resent her mother; she felt unwanted by all. She saw it in everyone's eyes, in their silent, gloomy faces. She knew it was a matter of time till their gloom turned into anger, and anger dried out their patience. Days passed, lonely and silent, till a whole year passed. It was a moonless night, like when she lost him, and the wolves returned. Late at night, she heard them howl, and the howling got closer and closer. She tucked baby Isabella in bed with shaky arms, locked her wagon and held a knife with a sweaty hand. The howling stopped, but she heard twigs cracking just outside her door. They were out there; she didn't know what to do other than stay still and quiet. Her wagon was parked away from the other wagons; she didn't expect help soon and couldn't shout for one. But then baby Isabella cried out loud, her mother tried to quiet her, dropped the knife, and held her, but she kept crying louder and louder. One of the wolves outside ran and banged into the wagon's door time after time. Isabella's mother held her tight in fear and cried out for help, but the wolf banged the door down and drooled at her doorstep. She gazed at it in fear but not for long. The wolf sprinted towards her with an open jaw; she curled on the floor, covering baby Isabella with her own body in protection. She felt the wolf's fangs bite into her back. All she cared about was protecting Isabella until help arrived, and she did; they reached her wagon and axed down the wolf, but it was too late for her. She gave her own life to save Isabella's. They tried to hunt the other wolf down but failed, it was strong and fast, and they ran out of breath as they watched it run deep into the woods.

Isabella was taken care of; everyone looked after her and ensured the baby girl didn't stroll alone into the woods. They hid her whenever they heard a wolf howl. The curse was intense and persistent; they had to travel more, one place after another, crossing hills, valleys, and rivers, until one day, the howling stopped. For many nights the howling stopped. They reached the furthest land they could reach, and they camped there. They camped at World's Edge.

Early in the morning, little Isabella strolled off camp, everyone was so tired and sleepy, but she was playful, curious, and stubborn. She crossed the woods and reached the village. The nearest cottage to the woods was of a simple old farmer who lived with his wife alone. They never had any children, their hair had turned grey years ago, and they knew they would never have any. They accepted it, but they never were truly happy because of it. The old farmer felt sorry for his wife because he left her alone in the cottage every morning and went to farm the fields all day long. That morning he found Isabella wandering around, strolling in front of the cottage. She wasn't from the Village. He noticed from her clothes that she was a gipsy, a beautiful gipsy child. Her pretty face, dangling earrings, hair braids and ballerina shoes at such a young age made her irresistibly adorable. She smiled at him, and his heart smiled back. He took Isabella's hand, carried her back to the woods, and found the camp. He asked for her mother and father, but they told him wolves had killed both. Touched at heart, the farmer kissed Isabella on her forehead and handed her to the gipsies. She hardly let go of him and cried hard as he walked away. He couldn't leave hearing her crying and seeing her stretching her arms out for him. He stopped, turned back, and spoke with emotions.

"I could take her to my wife. She could look after Isabella all day and keep her safe in our cottage. She spends the day with nothing to do. She will be glad to look after her if you don't mind. We will be more than happy to help." He had no idea what he was doing or saying, but the words just came out. He felt he was making a fool, maybe even offending the gipsies, but it was too late to step back now, and he had to wait for their answer. After a moment that felt like a decade to him, they surprisingly agreed. He couldn't imagine why; he didn't know that they thought Isabella might be safer with him at the cottage. They hoped that if she stayed there for a while, the curse might lose track of her, and the wolf would never find her again. They gave him Isabella and sent her clothes to the cottage. He was delighted; his wife loved Isabella like her own; they cared for her, nurtured her, played with her, loved her, and she loved them back.

When it was time for the gipsies to travel and carry on their endless journey, the farmer and his wife were devastated, and Isabella didn't want to leave. She cried out and held on firmly to the farmer's wife, they even tried to pull her away gently, but she never let go. The farmer took a leap of faith and asked the gipsies if Isabella could stay with them, live with them, have a new family, and promised to treat her like his own. Pressured by the moment, the gipsies gave thought to leaving Isabella and providing her with a new family; maybe it is safer for her, especially since the wolf didn't show up here at all, maybe it is the right thing to be done; and she was meant to be here, in World's Edge. They saw the amount of love Isabella held for the old farmer and his wife and believed maybe one of the travellers was meant to settle down. The gipsies allowed the old farmer and his wife to raise Isabella after agreeing they would stop by to check on her yearly during the full moon festival. They also stressed that she was free to leave the cottage and rejoin the tribe anytime she wanted to.

Delighted, the farmer gave the gipsies his word, and they shook hands on it. "She is in safe hands," he assured them as he and his wife cried happy tears and held Isabella closely. And so, there she was, the village's gipsy girl. Year after year, the gipsies stopped by every full moon festival and opened their arms to Isabella, but she never chose to leave her new family. She settled down; she remained a gipsy at heart, though. The way she dressed, her stone rings, earrings and ballerina shoes screamed gipsy. She grew beautifully, femininely, with a glowing smile, curly black hair and sparkling black eyes complimented by long eyelashes, a brunette with freckles all over her nose and dimpled cheeks. Her features were a mixture of the most admirable. She captured hearts so easily, one after another and out of all the hearts she captured, she captured the Merchant's heart.

He ran and ran, with no receptions, no protocols, no gifts for kings or queens. It was just Isabella and only Isabella on his mind and heart.

He found her walking on the roads of the old village, carrying a basket full of red roses.

"Isabella," the Merchant called out her name as he approached her; she instantly turned around and stunned him with a smile.

"I have missed you," said the Merchant as he held her close to him. She wrapped her arms around him.

"I've missed you, too," she said.

Noticing the basket hanging off her arm, he asked, "Are you selling these?"

"No," she said with a smile, stepped back and walked away in light steps. The Merchant caught up with her, "Where are you going?" he exclaimed.

"Come along. You'll see."

The Merchant followed her silently, but his thoughts grew loud. He felt like shouting his words, but he knew it was no use, for he already knew the answer to all his questions. They were in love, but she had never given in to him. Their relationship felt like a chase, committed but not submitted. Close, but not touching. Yet never broke up. She never pushed him away, yet never let him in. It was agonising, but he loved her; the more he knew her, the more he loved her. A daring gipsy flame that never failed to heat his passion. A stubborn wild beauty of nature, he would never stop chasing and loving. He followed her, watched her and everything he saw watered the deep roots of her love in his heart.

She walked to the elderly and poor sitting on the narrow roads of the old village and handed out the red roses, handing one rose to each with a warm smile.

"What are you doing?" asked the Merchant as he walked next to her while she continued handing out roses.

"Well, I usually give them bread, but today I don't have any to give," she answered.

"Isabella, my fleet will dock soon, and they will be given

gold and silver coins; you don't have to..." he said before she interrupted him.

"Stop it. Not again!"

"I mean, I can take care of the poor, Isabella, and you know that."

"I know you can take care of them, of their needs, of the ones who can run to the docks, but look," she pointed at an old blind woman touching the rose and smiling, "I also take care of their hearts,"

"Well then, what about taking care of my heart too, Isabella?" he said as she gave out the last rose and turned to him.

"And what would be of help?"

Here the poor cheered and ran past them to reach the docks and get help from the Merchant's fleet.

"You know Isabella, come with me," the Merchant shouted through the crowds flocking between them.

"No," she firmly answered, "not before you tell me." She insisted.

"I told you, Isabella. I told you!"

"You didn't tell me everything!" She blamed him and then walked off the roads, making her way back to the cottage on the green grassy hills.

The Merchant ran after her and held her arm to stop her from walking away, "You know I can't tell you everything; what I told you was enough!"

"Enough? Do you expect me to come with you, leave everything and everyone behind, hand you my life, and join your world without knowing everything about you? Without knowing where are you from? How did you get all this," she pointed at the fleet. She stepped close and held his face in her hands, "without even knowing your real name? I must know the man I am in love with. I need to fall in love with who you are, not whom I think you might be. I need to know!"

"You know I love you," he said.

"And I love you, but not fully, and I want to love you fully, and I can't fully love you without fully knowing you." She took her hands off her face and added I can't...I just can't," disappointed and hurt, she stepped back, and anger crawled up her face.

"If you want me to love you, then you have to be real to me; I am not going to fall in love with some fleet, even if it was a thousand ships, even if it was the Merchant's." She walked out, didn't turn around, didn't run back. She walked out.

Chapters 20

Clouds layered heavily over the sea. The sun was gone, and it was getting cold. The old Keeper stopped telling the story, stood up and walked to a small closet, picked up some wool clothes and turned to the sailor, "Put these on; you need heavier clothes,"

"But I have some already," the sailor reached for his bag, but the old Keeper tossed the clothes in the sailor's lap and said, "You'll need more, trust me; it never hurts to have extra warm clothes!"

"But what about you?" asked the sailor.

"Me? Don't worry, I have plenty of clothes." the old Keeper said as he lit a small hand lamp and placed it on the wooden table in the middle of the room.

"Don't you get lonely here? How do you stand being here all alone?" exclaimed the sailor.

"The sea is open, and so is my door. Ships pass by; I meet some people. Believe it or not, I always have something to do. It keeps me busy and from getting lonely. I fix things, I read, I write, I paint, I think, I always have something to do every day." He stared out the window. "But today," he sat back on his chair, wrapped a blanket around him,

"Today, I tell a story."

Chapter 21

After seeing Isabella, the Merchant went to see the old King. Of all kings the Merchant visits, the old King insists on receiving the Merchant himself. Waiting for his arrival at the castle's gate, every time, regardless of his ailing health and weak legs, in slow steps, he walked to the gate and welcomed the Merchant.

The guards announced his arrival, and the Merchant quickly walked straight to the old King.

"I am grateful for your generosity, Your Grace," said the Merchant.

"How could I not welcome you back myself? You are like a son to me," said the old King as he opened his arms to the Merchant. He was a lone King, last of his house, with no sons nor kin. His castle was small and humble, just like the whole kingdom, with a small village, a small fleet, and a small army. The only factors that kept this small Kingdom safe were its remote location and the weapons it had. Their weapons were unbreakable yet light. They made them out of a unique metal that can only be found in their lands.

"Is it ready?" the Merchant asked anxiously.

"It is ready, it is ready," smiled the old King as he signalled to the Merchant to follow him inside the castle.

The Merchant and the old King walked to the stables, where several rectangular wooden boxes were stacked over one another.

The old King nodded, and the guards opened one of the boxes, and as soon as they did, the Merchant's eyes were dazed by the beauty of what was inside. He had never seen such swords; he lifted one; it was light and long, made of some blue metal alloy; the swords were shining even though they stood in the shade.

"You can split a rock into two with one of these," said the old King.

"What about the spears and arrows?" the Merchant asked.

"Not ready yet...but will be," answered the old King.

"The liquid you gave us was useful. It made our already strong weapons stronger when we added them to the alloy. They are indestructible, oh that reminds me... how could I've forgotten... these swords must be treated first before use, or else they will rust and weaken like any other. They are fine here on land but can't be taken to sea for a long time. The swords must be treated first."

"Treated? How?" asked the Merchant.

The old King took out a small sack from the Swords' box, took a handful of some green powder out of it, and turned the Merchant.

"Bury it in the sands..." his cough interrupted his words, then he continued.

"Bury the weapons with some of this powder but keep the hilt up and exposed to the salty air and sunlight for seven whole days," said the old King.

"Sunlight?" exclaimed the Merchant, "the sun rarely

shows up from behind the clouds that shade World's Edge!"

"Find a place whose people you can trust..." the old King coughed a couple of more times then continued, "a sunny place, but keep the swords in the boxes till you get there, travel with them sealed," he added, holding back more coughs.

The Merchant then took a small bottle out of his pocket and said, "Here, this will help you clear your chest." He handed it to the old King, who in turn sipped a couple of droplets out of it.

"Thank you," said the old King, who sounded relieved immediately.

"The only kingdom with a sunny shore whom I can trust are the Silvers, but they are months away. If so, I must leave now to catch the sun," the Merchant said.

"Then do," said the old King.

"But the arrows and the spears are not ready yet," the Merchant remarked.

"It will be ready when you get back. Leave immediately, bury the blades, and come back for the arrows and spears."

The Merchant went into deep thought. It wasn't the effort of a short stay and the long journey back and forth that the Merchant was thinking about. It was her; he was thinking about Isabella.

Chapter 22

That night, the whole village gathered in the square. It was crowded, it was the gipsies' full moon festival, and everyone gathered around the large bonfire to see Isabella dance. She made her way to the centre through the crowd and stood in front of the bonfire. She looked captivating, with two blue ribbons in her hair, a full-length checkered red and white skirt, a white cotton peasant blouse, a burgundy coloured scarf, a black belt, and ribboned ballerina shoes. She stretched one leg and bent forward, leaning her hands on her foot, holding a moon-shaped tambourine. Her curly hair covered her face, she stayed still, and everyone was so quiet they heard the bonfire crackling.

The Merchant stood over the green hills watching Isabella with his eyes and heart. It was a fresh and beautiful night; the dew covered the grass, and the sea breeze blew gently under the full moon.

Isabella started to tap on the tambourine as she raised her head slowly with every tap, and when she fully stood up, she raised her tambourine and rattled its jingles rapidly, then stopped and looked down. The crowd cheered, and the music started playing. She danced round the fire; her gipsy blood flamed her moves, her hair complemented her steps, her eyes captured hearts, her smile captured souls. She swirled and swirled...while the Merchant stood still, uphill, watching, thinking. His thoughts rushed, and his feelings grew stronger. She danced, she smiled...then there it was...one clear feeling, one strong urge, one step after another downhill...the Merchant made his way through the crowd, broke the circle, and he reached her, grabbed Isabella from her waist away from all the people...took her up the green hills overlooking his fleet and the village. The music played on. He stood in front of her under the moonlight; she stared at him panting her breath.

He looked her in the eye. "So, if you want to know everything, I will let you know; you will know."

The Merchant grabbed Isabella and held her close to his chest, rested his chin over her shoulder and whispered; he rambled on, telling her everything, his deepest secrets, his best and worst, he told her everything. She listened carefully as he whispered. Her eyes reflected what he told her; she smiled at first, then looked worried, shocked, then afraid. He kept whispering, she panicked and tried to break away from his arms, but in turn, he held her stronger and whispered more. She tried to push him away, but he kept on whispering. She stopped struggling, she calmed down, her eyes filled up with compassion, tears and love filled her eyes, he whispered, she wrapped her arms around him then held him tightly, ran her fingers through his hair, her eyes started to shed tears, he whispered, she looked up the sky. He stopped whispering, stepped back, looked her in the eye and said,

"Well, that's me... now you know Isabella, you know

everything you wanted to know, and I know...I know that you are not perfect, and you could never be...I know that you are not all roses and cream; you are not as delicate as a butterfly or sweeter than honey...I know it is just YOU, and I love you. I know that you are not the most beautiful one in the world...but nothing in the world is beautiful without you."

He opened his arms wide, and she ran to him, rested her head over his shoulder and closed her eyes. He held her... she didn't let go...he carried her... went downhill, walked to the shore...and off to the sea.

)))

Chapter 23

The Merchant took Isabella's hand and walked her around the main deck. She couldn't believe it. The ship's main deck was greater than anything she imagined it would be. He showed her his house, not a cabin as she expected but a two-floor house. He showed her the baking area, the barns, the poultry, and the kettle ships. It indeed was like a small village floating on water. They moved from one ship to another using planks and lines. She was very excited. At some point, she slipped her hand out of his and skipped in front of him like a little girl, smiling back at him from time to time, and he knew it...she stunned him; she owns his heart, for she is like no other she is...Isabella.

"I could have never imagined this," she said.

"Welcome to Venus," said the Merchant as he took her hand to Venus' main deck

"So, the stories are true. It is a village on waters," she said.

"Is it also true that your fleet never breaks up even in the worst storms? It holds formation no matter what?"

"Yes, all of my ships always hold formation," answered the Merchant.

"How?" she exclaimed.

"Skilled sailors and fine ships," the Merchant smiled at her.

"And...is...it...true...that you have never let any woman

board the ship before?" she asked, afraid of hearing a disappointing answer.

"No! No woman has ever boarded Venus, never...only you. It has always been you. I was just looking for you, and now you are finally here," he answered as she smiled at him radiantly. The Merchant grabbed her waist," and some other stories are also true." The Merchant spoke gently in her ear.

"What other stories?" she looked at him in admiration.

"Come...I will show you. You must see it for yourself," the Merchant said as he walked Isabella down to the lower deck, they kept climbing down the stairs one floor after another until they reached the lowest deck.

The Merchant opened a door with a golden key he took out of his belt and walked her in. It was dark inside; she couldn't see anything.

"Where are we?" she asked.

"Wait," answered the Merchant, then lit a lamp with a match, he held it up for her to see around her, and what she saw astonished her... she saw gold...more gold than she'd ever seen or thought she'd ever see, not even in her wildest dreams, the whole lower deck was full of gold. Chests full of gold coins, stacks of gold bricks, pillars of pure gold, all pure gold.

"Welcome to Venus' Belly," said the Merchant proudly as he stood behind Isabella,

"You must be the richest man in the world," Isabella said without blinking.

"I am all yours, Isabella," the Merchant said as he held Isabella from the back tightly, "all yours" The Merchant then walked to a nearby chest, opened it and took a tiara out of it and placed it on Isabella's head,

"What's that?" smiled Isabella.

"It's yours. It is your crown," he said.

"Crown? Crowns are for kings and queens, and I am not a queen." she humbly said as she took it off her head.

The Merchant smiled at her with love and said, "place the tiara back on your head. You are a queen now, Isabella; you are my queen."

She looked him in the eye and stepped so close to him, and said,

"You don't have to give me all these gifts, for it is not what you place on my head or around my neck or on my fingers that matters to me, but it is what you put in my heart, and you have given love like nothing or no one I have ever loved."

The Merchant took the tiara from her hand and placed it on her head as he gazed into her eyes with love.

"Even if it were made of straws, I still would have worn it...because it is a gift from my one only from my love... from you," Isabella said as she dove into his arms and closed her eyes.

Chapters 24

The First Man ensured that every sword box was loaded on the ships.

The fleet was now ready to leave World's Edge and return to the Red Marbled Kingdom. He felt contradictory feelings. He is happy to see Prima again but also feels heavy at heart because he still can't be with her, win her. Marry her like the Merchant was marrying Isabella. After delivering the sword boxes, the fleet would return to World's Edge, and the Merchant would marry Isabella. She would wait for his return and prepare for the wedding where the Merchant will announce her Queen of the fleet. No woman had ever sailed the fleet, but the Merchant had made an exception for Isabella, and she would be joining the fleet, living aboard and sailing around the world.

"Wait for a second," he thought, "The Merchant made an exception!"

Relief started to lighten up his chest,

"Maybe he can make another exception for Prima. I can marry her against her stubborn father's will and live onboard, just like Isabella. I am the First man, after all. I am entitled to an exception too. The Merchant would agree; he will make the exception."

Hope made his assumption very convincing. The First Man smiled as he assured himself.

"The Merchant will understand and make the

exception... he definitely will."

The First Man's thoughts were interrupted by the Merchant's voice.

"All set?" asked the Merchant as he walked to him.

"That's the last box," the First Man pointed at the one being carried to the ship.

"And the powder?" asked the Merchant.

"All in," answered the First Man.

"Good! We will set sail at the break of dawn," said the Merchant.

"But won't we anchor for No land Day first, before we sail?" exclaimed the First Man.

"We don't have time. Sometimes we have to make an exception," answered the Merchant.

The First Man smiled with his heart and face.

"Yes...I believe so too...sometimes an exception has to be made."

The Merchant walked up the shore to his ship.

The First Man took a deep relaxing breath.

Chapter 25

During a standoff and a cold war between two kingdoms, spies became the most lethal weapon. No Silvers were allowed in or out of the Red Castle. Guards kept the borders and the gates tightly secured, especially the line, the borderline downhill that separated the two kingdoms. No one from either side was allowed to cross the line.

However, only one Silver hopped his way across the line freely. The guards helped him in and out, but behind their commander's back, that person was a kid, a sixteen-year-old...a mute kid.

The guards never considered him a threat because he was mute. To them, letting the Mute in and out was a simple breach of rules, not even a breach, just an exception that should take place behind their commander's back out of courtesy and nothing more. The main reason they did so is that the Mute smuggled in silver rings, silver bracelets and chains the Silvers were known for. He also delivered goods from the port. The Silvers' port was a commercial seaport, and none of the red guards had access to it. The Mute smuggled goods and sold them to the red guards, and he managed to set up his little black market that the red guards loved. They also loved him, he was funny, cheerful, and playful, and he always joked around and made them laugh. They never thought of him as a threat.

As usual, the Mute entered the red guard's barracks, sat on the ground, and laid all the goods on a piece of cloth for display. The Red guards chose what they liked and offered him a price. If the Mute accepts the price, he nods; if not, he shakes his head and waves his hand in rejection. The guards never wanted to upset or cut him an unfair deal because they knew the Mute would leave and never return if they did. He was their window to the world behind the seas.

That day, after he made his sales, the Mute packed and made his way back to the Silver Kingdom; just a few steps away from the red guards' barracks, the Commander and some Royal Guards showed up unexpectedly.

The Commander inspected the barracks inside out, looked at the gate and saw the Mute walking out.

"Who is that? What is that kid doing here?" the commander asked the guards suspiciously.

"Commander!" one guard exclaimed.

"I said, who is that? That boy. Who is he?" speaking firmly and pointing at the Mute.

"He is...he is...ah...he is just a trader, Commander." the guard stumbled with worry.

"A trader? Traders trade in the market... what is he doing here?" the Commander asked in a harsh tone.

"We buy some stuff...and..." the guard mumbled while the Commander eyeballed him closely.

"Commander," said the guard, "He is a mute kid," the guard justified.

"Mute or not, he still is a Sliver, isn't he?" the Commander clenched his jaw.

"Guards." In seconds the Royal Guards swarmed the place.

"Kill them all for treason." the line guards pulled their swords, and the fight began. "Traitors." he fumed out his anger, then turned to the Mute, who was now making his way uphill. The Commander grabbed a bow and arrow and aimed at the Mute.

The Mute was walking and hopping around the rocks, happy with the day's earnings. He didn't hear the arrow whistling through the air, but he saw it landing just next to his foot. The Mute gazed at it, then looked back in fear, and what he feared was what he saw, guards were being killed, and the Commander himself was taking another aim at him. The Mute instantly dropped his cloth sack and ran as fast as he could, zigzagging his way from the arrows that landed one after another just right next to his steps.

Suddenly he felt a terrible pain spiking in his back. He stopped, he knew it, he got hit by the Commander's arrow. The Mute fell slowly to the ground.

"To hell with your spies." the Commander said after making his catch.

The Silver guards were about to release their arrows in retaliation, but their officer shouted, "Hold your arrows. Hold."

The Sliver guards lowered their bows. "We don't want to start a war here," the silver officer said, ordering two guards, "Go get the child, lay down your weapons, go unarmed."

)))

Chapter 26

The Merchant's fleet sailed to the Sliver Kingdom. The First Man walked around Venus' main deck. It was about sunset; the breeze was light and fresh. He saw the Merchant leaning on the ledge, gazing at the horizon. The First Man walked to the Merchant and stood next to him.

"Homesick?" asked the First Man.

"Homesick?" exclaimed the Merchant, "the sea is my home!" he added.

"Home is where the heart is, and your heart is with Isabella back on land,"

"Well, she won't stay in World's Edge that long; we will drop the weapons and sail back right away...to her."

"Right back from the Silver port?" the First Man exclaimed, "won't we stop by the Red Kingdom as we always do?"

"Not this time. We'll greet them when we return to pick up the weapons from the Silvers' shore."

"Another exception then," said the First Man. He gathered his courage and said, "Well, I have been thinking; I mean, I wanted to ask you if... well...."

"What is it?" the Merchant interrupted

The First man looked at him and sighed, "Well. I am in love,"

"Who is she?" the Merchant asked.

"Prima," answered the First Man.

"The Minister's daughter? That is why you are eager to get to the Red Kingdom, right? But what did you want to ask me? Do you want off the fleet?" the Merchant asked.

"I have been in the fleet my whole life...leaving the fleet will be a tough step for me," said the First Man.

"Well, but it will happen sooner or later. Will it not?" said the Merchant.

"Well, someday, but I can't take this step now anyway, so I was wondering if you'd make another exception...for Prima and allow her onboard like...."

"As I did with Isabella?" the Merchant pointed out.

"Yes, exactly," said the First Man.

The Merchant paused for a moment, then looked the First Man in the eye and explained, "Isabella is just one exception...if an exception is to be repeated, it becomes a rule...and soon every man aboard will ask the same, and I do not intend to turn this fleet to a family packed carrier...I cannot help you with this. It is just out of the question. It could spin the whole fleet off balance," the Merchant cleared out.

Disappointment clearly showed on the First Man's silent face. The Merchant felt terrible for him, so he stepped in to find a solution. "I don't understand! Why do you want to board her? Why don't you settle with her on land...back at the Red Kingdom?"

"Her father, the Minister, refused me; he doesn't want me to marry her; I am not worthy enough from where he stands."

"So, take her away, go marry in some other land," the Merchant said.

"When it comes to his daughter, nowhere on land is out of his reach. He will reach us no matter how far we go. I will not be able to stop him from taking her back. After all, he is the Red Kingdom's Minister." The First Man smiled sadly, "But on the fleet, he can't touch us," he added, trying to convince the Merchant.

"Sorry to hear that, mate," The Merchant said to conclude their conversation and walk away.

"But there is another solution," the First Man said quickly.

"And what would that be?" asked the Merchant.

"If I am rich enough, her father will accept and bless our marriage. If I leave the fleet and settle down with Prima on land..., would I get my share of gold?" asked the First Man.

"Of course, like any one of the fleet men, you'll get a share of gold," The Merchant answered.

"No, that is not what I meant. I said my share of gold, not a share of the gold. I want my equal share of all the gold in Venus' Belly."

"What? an equal share? You know the rules. An equal is only given to the first man at the fleet's dismantlement. You know that! I can make sure to give you a hefty share of gold now, and if the fleet dismantles, I will bring you the rest of your equal share myself wherever you are. I have never broken a promise, and you know that everyone knows that, and that was the deal you agreed to since you joined my fleet. You don't need me to remind you, do you?" said the Merchant.

"No, I don't need a reminder, but matters are different now. Prima's father will only give me her hand in marriage if I prove to be rich," the First Man pleaded.

"Well, as I just said, I can make you rich with a hefty share of gold," said the Merchant as the conversation got tense.

"Yes, it will make me rich. Rich as any gentleman, but not rich enough to win her father's approval. If I get an equal share of gold, I'll be as rich as any nobleman. Only then can I buy a castle with vast lands, and Prima's father will be more than happy to give me her hand in marriage." The First Man protested the Merchant's offer.

With piercing eye contact, the Merchant reaffirmed, "A share of gold is all I can offer mate, a hefty share. If that doesn't work, you will have to find a solution. "The Merchant walked away to his deck house.

Disappointment fumed into frustration inside the First Man's chest. With the agony of being apart from his beloved, he got angry...he felt mad at everything...and everyone, especially the Merchant.

Chapter 27

Back in the narrow streets of the Silvers' village, in a poor small cottage, The Mute's mother dried the sweat droplets off his forehead. He'd been in and out of fevers, in and out of consciousness since that arrow from the back had wounded him. She watched him start to shiver. She gently touched his neck with her hand. The fever was getting higher and higher, and he began to mumble in his sleep.

She rushed to the table next to the bedroom window, picked up and opened a small crystal bottle containing an orange liquid; she dripped a few drops on the Mute's lips; he was breathing heavily and shivered more. She didn't know what else to do. She felt desperately helpless. That liquid was the only mean of help she had to keep her son alive, a medicine that the Merchant had given her long ago and instructed her to give any of her children in case they fell ill. she kept the bottle safe. It did come in handy and help keep her son alive despite his fatal wound, but it wasn't enough to heal him fully. She prayed with all her heart for the Merchant to come back soon. He is the only one who could heal her son.

She knew that she must patiently wait for the Merchant's return, but the medicine was running out, and so was her patience.

Chapter 28

The sea was calm at the edge of dawn, and the Merchant's fleet was quiet. Most of the crew were still in their cabins, including the Merchant. The main mast's man climbed up the pole quickly, grabbed one of the hanging horns up there, standing high overlooking the whole fleet, took a very deep breath in and blew the horn's sound. Everyone in or out of their cabins looked towards the sound in worry. Everyone knew what it meant. A crew member was dead.

The Merchant rushed out of his house and stood in front of it. He saw some gunner crew climbing up the stairs behind the house and striding towards him. They all looked sad.

"Who is it?" asked the Merchant to the one who approached him first.

"It is the head gunner, Merchant," he said.

The gravity of the loss showed on the Merchant's face. The head gunner was one of the oldest members of the Merchant's fleet. For years he had served the Merchant well with his top-notch fire skills. No one ran a fire floor as he did. He was old yet in good health; no one expected such sudden death. The Merchant felt taken by a sad surprise and troubled at the same time. Venus couldn't sail without a skilled head gunner, and he knew that none of the current crew could handle ninety guns on Venus alone as well as he did. Rearranging his thoughts, The Merchant exhaled a deep breath and commanded, "Anchor the ships and get ready for the funeral. Get Ji Kai".

Chapter 29

"Ji Kai?" the sailor asked the old Keeper.

"Yes. An old, old Chinese man. Traditional in every single way. Wise and calm, he always wore a complete traditional Chinese costume. No one in the Merchant's crew had been aboard before him. Some say he was the first one the Merchant recruited in his fleet. Some say he was more than a hundred years old but had the strength of a 20-year-old. He had very long hair, all white; it dangled from the top of his head to the back of his knees. Very quiet, rarely talked. He never shared a square or a bed with any of the sailors. He lived on a separate ship all alone. His mystical presence and old age made the sailors feel both curious and cautious around him. They would even avoid eye contact with him, but they often stared at him from a distance as he meditated every morning at sunrise.

"Ji Kai was the Merchant's head healer and oldest crew member, and he was the one to carry out funeral ceremonies," the old Keeper said.

"I bet their funeral ceremonies were different from all others," the sailor said.

"Yes. Very different. Very quiet," said the old Keeper.

"Do you know the details? Could you tell me all about it?" asked the sailor, who seemed very interested.

The old Keeper smiled lightly and nodded.

Chapter 30

The whole fleet anchored in the middle of the sea. All the high-ranking men in the Merchant's fleet lined up aboard Venus. All the gunners stood in a circle around the head gunner's body lying on a wooden table. After they washed him up and rubbed his body with rare aromatic oils, the Merchant stood alone on the plank. All other sailors watched from their ships. And they all waited for Ji Kai in silence.

In slow, steady steps, Ji Kai climbed the stairs behind the Merchant's house that led to Venus' main deck. As soon as he walked aboard, everyone standing in place took a step backwards as a sign of respect. Ji Kai walked and stood next to the head gunner's body, then took a small bottle out of his pocket, opened it, and handed it to one of the youngest gunners standing in the circle. He took the bottle from Ji Kai and whispered one word to the liquid inside it, then handed it to the one next to him. In turn, they all whispered a word to the bottle and passed it along until it returned to Ji Kai. He closed the bottle back, placed it in his pocket, then carried the head gunner's body with his arms, turned around, and made his way to the plank. At that point, everyone bent a knee and looked down, except the Merchant, who waited by the plank. Ji Kai stood before the Merchant and looked at the head gunner's body, all wrapped in linen.

The Merchant unwrapped the head gunner's head and exposed his face, then whispered a word in his ear. Ji Kai then walked the plank carrying the Head gunner's body, stood at the end, and rolled the body off his arms into the waters. As soon as the body splashed its way to the seabed, Ji Kai took out the bottle from his pocket, opened it and shook it empty into the same spot he dropped the body. Then he picked a long rope tied to the plank and threw its loose end into the waters. Ji Kai said words that no one understood as he threw the bottle far away into the sea. Everyone stared at the rope dangling from the plank into the waters. Dropping the rope was essential to their rituals, for the Merchant and his men believed that their souls would climb up the line back to the ship. "The Line", they called the rope, was their souls' way back to where it belonged to the fleet.

Slowly Ji Kai made his way back to his ship, and the Merchant walked to his house. The gunners carried the wooden table and walked back to their floors. Then everyone left Venus' main deck. The First Man was the last to leave.

Chapter 31

The Mute's mother sat on the edge of his bed. She felt helpless. Life was being drained slowly out of her son. The Merchant's medicine kept him alive for months, but she had just dripped the last of the liquid on the Mute's lips. Her tears broke and turned into weeping; she couldn't hold them back any longer. "I am going to lose him," she thought, "Is it my fault? Have I been a horrible mother to him? Should I have never let my twins spy? Even if it was for the benefit of the kingdom?"

Yes, the Mute had a twin; they were identical in every feature but one. He wasn't mute. They were both born with full hearing capability, but the second one caught a fever that almost took his life.

Nonetheless, the fever didn't spare his hearing. He grew deaf and mute. The Silvers thought it would be a great trick to play on the Reds. Send them the Mute first, as a trader, a smuggler, and when they rest assured that the boy couldn't hear anything around him and couldn't talk about anything he saw in the barracks of the Red Castle, his twin would replace him and switch them now and then. The trick worked out well for a long time. "But now my boy is dying, and I can't save him," the mother thought in agony.

"Mother," said her other son standing by the door.

She looked at him silently, but he soon broke the silence with the best news.

"He is here; the Merchant has arrived." She instantly cried out a happy tear while holding onto her son.

)))

Chapter 32
"The widow gave birth!"

"The widow gave birth," she remembered. She remembered people shouting that phrase every day, for how could she forget such a day? Such a moment when she gave birth to her twins. They handed her the twins, one after another, her tears pouring in sadness and happiness inside. She is now a mother of two wonderful boys and two orphans, for their father died in battle, defending the kingdom and protecting them. She never wished to have him next to her as much as she did that day. That moment when she heard people shouting, "The widow gave birth." She felt helpless and fragile, insecure, and anxious, but she toughened up to raise them on her own. But now and then, she broke down, and only one man lifted her back to her feet at such moments. The Merchant was her backbone, caretaker, and saviour. At the darkest times, he was her only light. The Merchant even taught the Mute a language, a sign language through which he could communicate and express himself. He taught both of her sons at a very young age. The Mute waved the words, and his brother spoke them out. She still remembered the happy tears she cried when he waved his first sentence, and his brother translated it to her...the sentence was, "I love you."

The Mute's mother and brother ran to the docks

and were allowed onboard Venus. It was an impressive experience for anyone who dreamt of stepping aboard the legendary ship. Still, they were focused on the Merchant, awaiting his reply after the mother heartily asked for his kind help.

The Merchant waved to one of his men, and the man brought him a small wooden box in a moment. The Merchant opened the box. It had six small glass bottles just like the one she had, but each had a liquid of a different colour, red, yellow, green, purple, black and white.

"The healing will take time. He has been ill for quite a while. You won't be able to treat him yourself. It will be too confusing for you and too risky for the child," the Merchant said, then turned to the First Man who stood next to him. "The First Man will stay with you. He knows how to treat your son using the medicine correctly," then he looked the First Man in the eye. "Stay with her and heal the Mute till we get back."

"At your command," nodded the First Man. He felt happy to have the chance to see Prima yet wasn't entirely comfortable with the Merchant's decision. He could have left a healer to treat the Mute. The First Man was skilled, yes, but why him? And not a healer? Maybe it's a subtle penalty for crossing the line that day, or perhaps the Merchant is just giving him time to rethink it all with Prima.

"Thank you, Merchant, thank you so much," said the Mute's mother. The First Man accompanied her off Venus' main deck. She walked ahead, right in front of the First Man, who stood still for a moment and looked back at the Merchant.

The Merchant was leaning on the ledge, the sun was about to set, and the horizon was painted red. The Merchant watched the Silvers digging holes on the beach, emptying a handful of the green powder, sticking in the swords then filling the hole with sand. Hundreds of blades were buried to the handle all along the shore; it looked somewhat beautiful, yet intimidating, planted swords that only the reaper had to worry about. The First Man gazed at it all momentarily, and then he walked away. A sailor's heart could always sense when the winds were about to change. He walked along the shore, hearing the men shouting through,

"Set sail... set sail!"

Chapters 33

"**F**ather. The First Man wants to meet you," Prima said hesitantly to her father as they were having dinner at their humble house.

"Not again!" the Minister said as he put his spoon on the plate.

"Father, please. He is the one for me," she pleaded.

"Yeah, he is the one as you see him, but he is the wrong one from where I see it."

Prima almost left the table, but her father grabbed her arm.

"So, what do you want me to do? Stand with a smile as I watch my only daughter ruin her life for someone not worthy of her. Huh! is that what you want me to do? You are practically asking my permission to harm yourself, my only child."

"I am not harming myself...you are the one who is harming me," Prima said as she pulled her arm away.

"Me?" the Minister was shocked and in pain to hear it.

"Listen, darling," he stopped her.

"No, father, you listen! Do you believe that every woman who married a wealthy man is happy, and every other poor couple is not? When my mother married you, weren't you poor? Yet, she loved you; was she miserable? No, she was happy, wasn't she?" she burst into anger.

"But she ended up in misery!" The Minister shouted,

"no matter how much we loved each other, my love for her couldn't save her. She died because I couldn't afford to treat her. Love brought her to me; poverty took her away, and I will never let that happen to you."

"But we are rich; I don't need a wealthy man," she exclaimed.

"We are not rich enough, not powerful enough. We can't even buy a castle yet," he said.

"I don't want a castle, father; who said I want to live in a castle? I hate castles."

"Prima once and for all. You are not marrying that sailor, no matter how much you think you love him or how much you think you hate castles. Understood?" the Minister said firmly.

"All this because of what you think it is. All that because you think you know what is the best thing for me? You don't even know what the best thing is, father. If you have seen what I have seen in the hallows of that castle, you would have never said so, but I have seen the woman everyone thinks has it all. I have seen her cry in her sleep, the misery of loving one and living with another, and I will not let myself end up like that in some castle. I will not, and no one will force me to, not even you, father."

"What? what do you mean?"

"Nothing!''

He grabbed her, "Prima, what have you just said? Whom are you talking about?"

"Nothing I said," she yells as he tightens his grip around

her arm.

"Answer me!"

"Father, you are hurting my arm!"

"Answer me. Who is the woman you are talking about?"

"Father! Let go," she tried to slip away but couldn't.

"Answer me."

"The Queen! It is The Queen!" Prima said in defiance, "she doesn't love the Red King. She is in love with another man. She is heartbroken, and I will live like that if I don't marry the one I love."

"Whom? Whom does she love?"

"Father, let me go."

"Who is he?" he yelled at her.

"The Merchant...she loves the Merchant," Prima finally shouted.

The Minister let her arm go. She ran to her room, and he dropped his weight on the chair and went into a deep trance of sparking thoughts. He was overwhelmed, indeed. He finally did; such a thing was all he needed to hear for a long while. A smile drew itself on his face.

Chapter 34

The Red King lay on his back, waiting for the Queen to come to bed. He knew he had to wait for her to finish brushing her hair; taking good care of her long hair was a routine she never skipped, not any night.

"Can you imagine that the Merchant has docked at the Silvers' and left on the same day without stopping by the castle to greet us." the Red King said.

"That's a first," the Queen remarked, "but why is that? Did any of your spies know the reason? The Red King turned on his right side to face her, "Well, the word is he is getting married," The Queen stopped brushing her hair, "What?" she exclaimed.

"Can you imagine? He turned back on the same day just to be with her...to marry her. He is rushing back to his wedding. They say he is deeply in love with her, but of course, no one can love anyone as much as I love you," he said with a smile.

The Queen started to breathe heavily, "And... who is the lucky one?" she asked.

"A gipsy girl who lives far in World's Edge Kingdom. She will join the fleet. He put a tiara on her head and crowned her queen of his fleet!" The Red King laughed, "Can you imagine? A woman aboard the fleet. He is breaking the rules for her. He is down to his knees."

The Queen didn't join his laughter and seemed angry.

The Red King noticed and asked, "What's the matter? Are you all right, my love?"

"No. I am not," she sprung off her dresser's seat, "I will retire to my chamber," she said as she exited the royal suite. The Red King stared at the door after she slammed it behind her.

)))

Chapter 35

The First Man sat in front of the Minister at his humble cottage, and Prima sat midway on the long wooden table.

"Thank you for finally allowing me to meet you, Minister," the First Man said in a very insincere voice. The Minister replied with an ice-cold silent look.

At some point, Prima felt obliged to break the silence, "He...ah...is staying with us...on land...for some months... till," the Minister interrupted and stopped her sentence with a simple hand signal.

"So, you are the one who has my daughter's heart?" said the Minister in a subtle tone.

"She has my heart, too. We are in love and want to spend the rest of our lives together," the First Man said.

"Love isn't enough," said the Minister, then added, "marriage is like building a house; it can't be built on soft land. It would fall apart. The hard surface of the reality you are escaping is what holds mountains up. Fall in love, both of you, as much as you want, but if you want to sustain that love, to protect it, it must be sheltered by thick hard walls and trust me, those thick hard walls are costly."

The First Man leaned forward and said, "I understand that you want the best for Prima, and that's what I want for her too. I will do everything I can to be that 'best' for her.''

"And how do you intend to do that?" asked the Minister.

"Well, to begin with, I will leave the fleet, get…ah…a hefty share of gold then…ah…I…."

"What? What share? What gold?" the Minister interrupted the First Man.

"Yes! What gold?" Prima asked.

Now he's got their attention, the First Man eased up and smiled a little, then explained, "Every single trade the Merchant profits is shared, with all of his crew members in gold, and since I have been the fleet's first man for a long time, my share adds up enough to make me a wealthy man." he said. At the same time, the Minister sceptically stared at him. Prima smiled in relief and shook her head, "How come you never told me about this before?" She blamed the First Man.

"I didn't want to jump ahead before clearing it out with the Merchant himself. Just to be sure," the First Man justified.

"Well, that is good to hear, but how rich are we talking about here?" the Minister asked.

The First Man seemed a little worried and uncomfortable, answering, "Well, rich as we will have enough to start with."

The Minister leaned back on the chair. The First Man felt he was losing his interest, so he jumped up with more news, "But just for now, that is just a share; I'll be richer when I get my share, in full."

"What do you mean?" Prima asked while the Minister stared and listened.

"If the fleet is dismantled, I will get my full equal share.

An equal share of Venus's gold would make me as rich as the richest prince. There is enough gold in her belly to build a kingdom," the First Man stressed.

Suddenly, the Minister seemed amused and leaned forward on the table, "So the stories are true...Venus' fat Belly is loaded with gold," the Minister said.

"More than you can imagine," said the First Man as he held Prima's hand. She instantly smiled at her father with happiness in her eyes.

The Minister stood up, turned his back to them, seemed to be thinking, and then turned to the First Man. "Walk with me," he said to the First Man as he walked to the door and waited at its step, "Prima, wait for us here." he added.

The Minister and the First Man strolled around the cottage. After taking a few steps, the Minister started a conversation, "What did you mean by saying 'if the fleet is dismantled'?"

"Well, the Merchant has put some rules. There are certain conditions that, in some cases, dismantle the fleet. He doesn't intend to roam the seas forever after all," said the First Man.

"And what are those conditions?" asked the Minister.

"It is simple, either the Merchant orders the dismantlement himself or if...well I...I'd rather not speak about the other condition," the First Man answered.

"I bet the second condition has to do with the Merchant's death, doesn't it?" the Minister said.

The First Man smiled in compliment, "Yes, Minister, it

does. That's why I'd rather not talk about it."

"As you like. But you never know when?" the Minister mocked.

"When?" the First Man exclaimed.

"When would the Merchant ever orders the dismantlement?" said the Minister.

"No," the First Man answered abruptly, "But the Merchant has never broken a promise," he defended.

"A promise! With an open condition, it sounds like a fake promise to me." The Minister pointed, " and let me ask you this, have you ever seen the Merchant give out an equal share to anyone who has devotedly worked for him?"

"Not that I know of, but I am sure that...."

"And tell me, does that equal share excludes or includes Isabella's share now? I heard he's given her a tiara!"

The First Man answered in uncomfortable silence, and here the Minister continued, "Exactly," the Minister stopped and looked the First Man in the eye, "you are just finding comfort in the illusion of trusting the Merchant. A promise that has never been fulfilled and is left to sheer uncertainty is nothing but an illusion, and you are convincing yourself that such an illusion is real. Do you want me to leave my only daughter on the threshold of an uncertain future that will never be realised? if you want to marry Prima...get your equal share or get out of her life." The Minister walked back to the cottage.

"But the fleet has to be dismantled first!" the First Man spoke out of frustration.

The Minister stopped, turned around, walked to the First Man, and laid his hands over his shoulders, then spoke with a smile of confidence on his face, "I am a resourceful man, and I can help you get your equal share no matter what or even better, bigger than you so-called 'equal share'."

"What do you mean?" the First Man asked in a tense voice.

"No! That is not the question you should be asking now! What you should be asking is how deeply you love Prima. And how far do you trust the Merchant?" the Minister walked a few steps away from the First Man, then turned back to him and shouted, "and you know what I mean."

)))

Chapter 36

"The question you should ask is how deeply you love Prima? And how far do you trust the Merchant?" the Minister's words kept resounding in the First Man's head, "How deeply do I love Prima?" he thought, "what made me fall in love with Prima in the first place? She is pretty, yes, she is beautiful, but it is not just that. One woman's beauty is enough to grab a man's attention, but it is not enough to make him fall in love with her. It is not how she looked, but what she promised, yes, her beautiful face promised me beauty in every aspect, and she fulfilled that promise. Her warmth, passion, tenderness, and subtle allure are just beauty in manifestation. She is my mind's very definition of beauty. How could I give her up? How could anyone give up the beauty and drive it out of his life?

Beauty is the only thing we love, and wherever we see it, we hold on to it, whether it is a place, a thing, a state or atop of all, a person. Beauty is our only goal, all of us, but we just see it differently. 'How much do I love Prima?' he recalled the Minister's question. "Love! What is love? It is a feeling, no! It is the only feeling. We feel nothing but love. Hate is the opposite of love; pain is losing what you love, jealousy is not having what you love, and loyalty is committing to what you love. The Merchant once told me that all colours come from one single ray of white light.

Love is that white light for all our feelings. All our feelings are just a variation of love. Yes, we only feel love, and Prima is the only one I feel. That is how deeply I love Prima. That answers your question, minister," the First Man concluded.

"And how far do I trust the Merchant?" the First Man now thought, "he never broke a promise true, but he only fulfilled the promises he made of his perspective and judgment, and according to his judgment, I can't get my equal share, even though he knows that this means I would lose Prima, the love of my life! According to his judgment, he can make an exception for Isabella and crown her queen of the fleet, but I can't get my equal share even if my life depended on it. Selfishness is when one judges from his perspective only, which is what the Merchant always does. I trust him when it comes to keeping his promises, but I don't trust how he judges things! I guess now it is time for me to judge!"

Chapter 37

Late at night, Prima couldn't sleep, and her father couldn't either. She stepped downstairs and found him sitting in front of the fireplace staring at his late wife's face portrait. She looked beautiful in that painting.

"Sleepless?" he asked Prima, then took a sip of his drink.

"Yes." she smiled tenderly.

"You are sleepless here. You are sleepless in the Red Castle, till when Prima?" he said.

"I will sleep in the arms of the one I love," she answered; the Minister smiled slightly, then turned his eyes to the painting; he seemed very emotional at the moment.

"Do you still love her?" Prima softly asked.

The Minister sighed, and tears filled his eyes, "Every single moment I spend without her, I spend in agony. If it weren't for you, Prima, I wouldn't have been able to carry on," he said.

"I love you, father," he laid her hand on his arm.

"And I love you too, darling. And I want you to be happy and live in love, like your mother and I," he said.

"Do you?" she asked.

"I do. I do," he stressed, but she didn't seem entirely convinced, so he turned to her, "And I will help you," he stressed.

"Help me? How?" she exclaimed.

"I can help you be with the First Man by helping him

get his gold," he explained.

"Really," she smiled in relief.

"Yes, but first, I need you to get me something from the Red Castle."

"What is that?" she asked.

"You said that The Queen write love letters to the Merchant, right?"

"Yes, she does."

"And the Merchant returns those letters to her, right?"

"Right."

"Does she keep those letters somewhere, or does she burn them?" he asked, keen to hear the answer.

"No, she doesn't burn them. She keeps them hidden in her chamber," Prima answered, now expecting what will her father ask her to do.

"I knew she'd keep them! Well, do you know where she hides them? Can you get me one, just one of those letters?"

Prima seemed hesitant to answer, so he pressured her more.

"All I need is that one letter, and I will help you be with the First Man. He will be rich and wealthy then, and you both will have my endless blessing to your marriage."

Before Prima answered, they heard some loud knocking on the cottage's door.

"Who is that at such a late time?" Prima worried.
The Minister smiled confidently, "I bet I know who that is, and it is not too late. He is just in time." The Minister put down his drink, headed to the door, and opened it.

"Welcome...son," the Minister said to the First Man standing by the door.

)))

Chapter 38

The Black Collar entered the bar, nodded at the bartender, and walked directly behind the counter, through the door and down to the room below. The Minister was already there, waiting at the round wooden table. As soon as he heard the Black Collar enter, he spoke, "You are here," the Minister smirked.

"You wanted to see me 'urgently', I believe you stressed," the Black Collar said as he took off his coat and hung it.

"Yes," said the Minister, then added, "have a seat."

The Black Collar sat in tense anticipation. He was fed up with the Minister's prolonging games he always played to buy himself more time.

"What did you want to see me for? Do you have a plan?" asked the Black Collar.

"I want to see...the Dean," said the Minister.

"What now?" the Black Collar smirked back.

"You heard me," the Minister said confidently.

"And why do you want to meet the Dean? If you don't mind me asking, Minister!"

"He will know himself when he gets here," said the Minister.

"What? Are you out of your mind? Not only do you want to see the Dean in person, but to top it off, you want the Dean himself to come to you?" the Black Collar ridiculed.

"Yes," answered the Minister calmly.

The Black Collar paused as he noticed how calm and confident the Minister was.

"Even if I asked him to, how would I convince the Dean to come to you here?" he asked the Minister. "Tell him that…this is it. This is when and where we bring down the Merchant once and for all," answered the Minister.

"Do you have a plan?" asked the Black Collar. The Minister smiled and seemed even a little happy, then said, "I have what's better than a plan. I have an ally from the inside. Tell the Dean that the Merchant is stronger than each of us, but he is not stronger than all of us, but for all of it to happen, he has to be here, and it has to be now."

Chapters 39

Two veiled men lay atop the highest hill and shared a telescope to look at the swords spiked along the Silvers' shore. After taking a good long look at them, one of the veiled men put down the telescope, looked to the other and left...a moment later, the other man followed.

The Red King and the Minister removed their veils as they entered the royal hall. The Red King sat on the throne and signalled for his drink.

"Why haven't you told me earlier?" the Red King asked.

"I wanted you to see for yourself, Sire," the Minister replied with a nod.

"So? I did," the Red King said just before sipping his drink.

The Red King's cold comment triggered the Minister's temper

"He is arming them, Sire...The Merchant is arming the Silvers!" the Minister stressed out.

"No... you said the weapons are the Merchant's, not theirs. He didn't sell it to them, and even if he is arming them, no matter how strong those swords are, we will still crash them to the ground if they ever roll downhill."

"Why are you doing this? Sire," said the Minister to the Red King, stepping a little off protocol.

"Doing what, Minister?" answered the Red King in a deeper voice as if warning the Minister not to step too far offline.

"This! You do it every time, your Highness. You find him a way out, an excuse...as if you never want to confront him."

"Have you lost your mind?" yelled the Red King.

"May I speak to you in private?" asked the Minister.

"Speak to me in private? At this point, I wonder if I should allow you to address me at all," said the Red King.

"Your Highness, I beg you." pleaded the Minister.
The Red King had never seen such an act from the Minister. So, he signalled the guards and servants out of the royal hall. As soon as the last one left and shut the door, the Red King burst into anger, "Are you testing my patience? Because if you are, I must warn you, I have none."

"So why are you that patient with the Merchant?" asked the Minister.

The Red King gazed, "Again? Why does this matter to you that much? What difference does it make anyway?"

"You know what the difference between him and us is?" asked the Minister,

"What?" asked the Red King impatiently.

"Them!" The Minister pointed outside the windows. "Them, the people, the guards, the Silvers, the children, all of them! They love him more than anyone of us...more than you, your Highness, more than the Queen herself... they talk about him, praise him...wait for him by the shore...he owns them. They are his. He sails the sea with an army bigger than any on land. He has weapons that no one can beat...weapons made of metal no one has seen before. He has enough cannons to light up the night sky. 'What is the matter of all that? Where is it going?' You ask me, Sire! But I ask, would he keep roaming the seas, cure people, and help everyone without asking for anything in return? No, Sire, of course not. He is just waiting for the right moment. He has already won...strategically, he has already beat our soldiers with his, beat our cannons with his, and when the time is right, he will take over the Kingdom with a snap of his fingers, and you know what? They...they won't mind... because they love him, Sire. Throughout my serving years, I have learnt that one shouldn't fear the strongest in arms but rather the most loved in hearts. The hearts of your enemy, the hearts of your people and above all, the heart of all hearts...the heart...of your Queen."

The Red King was shocked, and the Minister instantly laid the Queen's love letter to the Merchant.

The Red King picked up the letter; he didn't say a single word; he just read the letter with gazing eyes, disbelief, anger, and embarrassment. He walked back to his throne and sat down. He seemed unable to hold himself up any longer. The Minister took the opportunity of the moment.

"Let's take him down, Sire. Let us break him once and for all and end all this...," the Minister said.

The Red King looked at him with blurry vision while the Minister continued to pressure an approval.

"I have a plan...no matter how strong he is, no matter how many men he has or how strong his weapons are, I have a plan to bring him down. I've always planned to protect your throne. I have always looked after your crown and your father's. The Red Crown shall prevail by the loyalty of its followers always."

The Red King kept staring at the letter in his hand.

"There is a force in the blind spot, one the Merchant does not account for. I had to find a new, unexpected way to make the plan. After all, the enemy of our enemy is a friend. Hundreds of pirate ships are on the seas; one thinks they are astray, but they are all governed by one family... and I have established contact with them. Of course, they are the only ones who can bring the Merchant down in return for a mutual benefit. They are named The Blacks, Sire."

Still, the Minister got no reaction from the Red King. It was as if his mind was locked in limbo.

"I know it is overwhelming, Sire...all at once...you need to take your time, but let's not lose our opportunity here, for the Merchant's first man is on the ground, he is on our side...he even wants to bring the Merchant down. See? even the closest to the Merchant knows the threat he imposes," the Minister paused, then added, "I will be in my house, Sire. Make your decision, and I will be at your service. But for now, I highly suggest that no one knows anything about this, not even the Queen, especially the Queen."

Then the Minister walked out, leaving behind The Red King alone in the Royal Hall. The Minister walked out with a smile on his face.

Chapter 40

The Red King stayed in the Royal Hall until the next day. He didn't sleep, didn't eat, didn't drink, and didn't allow anyone in.

At the break of dawn, he called in his guards and asked them to summon the Minister, who rushed to the Red Castle and stood in front of the Red King.

"Sire," he said, but the Red King didn't answer back and was still staring at the letter in his hand as he stood by the narrow window.

"Shall I call the Blacks?" the Minister asked, but still, the King didn't turn or answer back. He stood there silently, gazing into an infinity of his mind. Anger seemed to pressure his veins under his skin and push his mind to insanity.

The Minister hesitated to ask again because he had never seen the Red King that angry, silently angry. Still, the opportune moment gave the Minister enough courage to raise his voice and ask the Red King again...

"My King, shall I call for the Blacks?"

All the Minister was waiting for was a simple nod to set his wicked plan into action. The Red King nodded.

The Minister smiled and raised his chin; he couldn't hide the thrill and pride of his cunning wits.

The Red King watched the Minister walk out of the throne hall to call for the Blacks, but the Red King didn't know that a black carriage pulled by four black horses made its way through the mists of the woods. A black carriage topped with a black feathered crow, beak down, wings spread, the unmistakable crest of a family that has long worked in the shadows. The Red King didn't know that the Blacks were already on the way.

Chapter 41

The black carriage stopped and hid in the woods while the Minister sneaked out of the Red Castle and ushered the unannounced guest into the Royal Court. The Red King's unannounced guest was the Black family's Dean himself.

The Dean was an arrogant, egoistic, powerful, middle-aged man. Though they should have been the eldest to be dean of the family, he became dean because he was the most cunning, ruthless, manipulative man in the Black family. His looks also gave him the aura he needed to rule the family, an Albino with white skin, white hair and piercing blue eyes that one would instead not dare to look to. He always dressed in black and wore the Black family's crest ring on his right index finger, a black ring made of black metal shaped like the image of a black crow.

The Red King received the Dean in a secret meeting room in the Red Castle. They sat face to face and waited for the Minister to usher in the one person left who needed to attend and start laying out the plan. The Minister smiled as he opened the doors and presented their most vital ally.

"This is the Merchant's first man," he introduced him.

The First Man seemed a little tense and hesitant to make such an alliance, but as soon as he sat with them at the same table, he dived in headfirst and said, "I want half."

"Half?" the Minister exclaimed.

"Half of the gold," the First Man cleared.

"And why do you think you are entitled to half of the earnings?" the Dean asked the First Man, with non-blinking eye contact.

"Because it is not half of the earnings. When the Merchant is brought down, the seas will be open for your pirate ships, and you will make tons more than what you are making now." Then he looked at the Red King. "When the Merchant is out, you will be able to rebuild the ships and take the furthest corner of the world under your sovereignty. The Red Kingdom will be the largest in the world, and you," he turned to the Minister, "you will be the minister of such kingdom." Then he turned to the three of them, "You will all have that, plus your share of gold, but I will only get the gold, so I am 'entitled' to half of the gold because half of the gold is not half of the earnings." The First Man answered the Dean's question.

"You are correct," said the Dean, "in case you are the only way to bring down the Merchant, but I hear could be other ways, too. Other cheaper ways," he added.

"What other ways? Attack the fleet, shoot your cannons?" the First Man ridiculed.

"Yes. I believe all our pirate ships, all the Red Kingdoms' cannons, if placed on the teardrop isles, would form a colossal fire force that could drown the Merchant's fleet, yes." said the Dean arrogantly.

The First Man smirked, "But by then, you will not get the gold to cover the expenses; making such an attack is too expensive for you to carry out without my help."

"What do you mean?" asked the minister.

"If what the Dean is saying works and your cannons drown the Merchant's fleet, you would lose the gold forever because Venus' Belly is not made of wood like the rest of the ships. It is made of steel," the First Man answered back.

"Steel?" finally breaking his silence, the Red King commented.

"Yes, your Grace, steel. The Belly is made from a steel chamber that, if drowned, the water pressure turns a lock that only the Merchant has the key to. No one knows where he keeps the key or even what it looks like. If the Belly is locked underwater, we will not be able to pull it out. The gold will stay in the locker forever." The First Man then stood up, looked the Dean in the eye, and said, "I know the fleet, I know the men, I know their code and protocols, I know how to get you the gold because I...I am the First Man!"

Chapters 42

"The lighthouse...always a place of fascination," the sailor thought to himself as the old man paused to sip his soup with a shaky spoon. The sailor smiled as he noticed that he had never been in a lighthouse before, having seen many but never entered any. "What a first!" he thought to himself, then said to the Keeper, "Thank you for the soup. It was delicious." The Keeper didn't reply, didn't look at him; the old man just sipped his soup rhythmically. The Sailor then sat quietly, passing the time by watching the heavy cold weather outside.

When the Keeper finished his soup, he set the plate aside, rubbed his mouth with a piece of cloth, and then popped, "I forgot! I knew that I forgot a part!"

"What's that?" asked the sailor.

"I forgot a part of the story", he answered.

"It's all right. What part?" said the sailor.

"PaleFace, after the Merchant's head gunner, passed away, the Merchant tested each of the gunners in his crew, but no one was up to the standard. See, Venus' fire force was fierce and heavy to handle. Not just because it had too many fire floors and too many cannons, no, it was...tricky... the mechanism was unique and easily confusing."

"How?" asked the sailor.

"The cannons were connected; every four cannons were attached and were loaded and fired all together at the same time. They were retracted, ejected, or switched from star to port sides by a hand leveller, so the head gunner had to memorise the fire pattern of all fire floors, synchronise them, and cue the firing, especially since not all the cannons on Venus had the same range," the Keeper explained.

"Oh boy, that sounds confusing, but how would the main gunner communicate with all fire floors?" asked the sailor.

"Through copper tubes, he shouted his command in a tube, and each floor had a Listener who shouted the command repeatedly to the fire crew. The head gunner had a control spot on the top fire floor with all the copper tubes and levellers. That's why they all called him Top Gunner. After the Merchant tested all the gunners, he couldn't find one that fit until he tested one man, not from the crew, but from shore, a man who was on a ship he had rescued from pirates, a man who was on the captain's ship but never sailed back with it, he stayed in the silver harbour. A man who was known by the name PaleFace."

Chapter 43

After recruiting PaleFace, leaving the First Man behind, and digging the swords in the Silvers' shore, the Merchant sailed back to the Kingdom of World's Edge, where his beloved Isabella was preparing for the wedding.

After the wedding, for the first time, the Merchant docked his fleet for a whole month and took Isabella to some hidden tropical island where they ate nothing but fruits and honey. They manifested their love in every dance, every touch, every smile, and every hug, away from everyone. They were the happiest because all they wanted and needed was each other and only each other. But the moon was darker on the other side. While the Merchant was gone for months, the Dean, the Minister, the Red King, and the First Man laid a carefully plotted plan to bring the Merchant down. Every time the First Man hesitated, Prima jolted him back on track. So, he gave them every detail they needed, every weakness, every flaw, every secret. To him, it was all about winning Prima; that is what numbed his conscience and warmed his heart. Wining Prima was all there was, and nothing else mattered.

Chapter 44

Crowned queen of the Merchant's fleet, Isabella never took the tiara off her head. The months she spent aboard was the happiest she'd ever been throughout her whole life. She was finally with the one she loved the way she loved. She knew him, truly understood the Merchant like no one other did. She held his secrets, his heart, and his, and she was in love with him, and it was real, just real solid love.

After a long journey back to the Silver and Red Kingdom, the Merchant's fleet finally reached the silver port. Skipping greeting the Red King on his last visit, the Merchant determined to see the Red King first, out of courtesy.

The Red Kingdom's guards lined up on the beach, the customary lineup of receiving the Merchant and announcing his arrival, "The Merchant, " they announced aloud. Still, the Merchant asked the guards to repeat the announcement, mentioning Isabella.

"The Merchant..." the guards seemed hesitant to finish the announcement, but they couldn't ignore the Merchant's request, "the Merchant and... his Queen," they shouted. Back at the Red Castle, the Queen heard the announcement and jumped off her seat, furious at what she had heard " What? I am the Queen. I am the only Queen," she yelled.

"Welcome, dear friend," said the Red King to the

Merchant as he entered the Royal Hall with Isabella holding his hand.

"Ah...so this is the beautiful one we've been hearing about," said the Red King as he looked at Isabella in an over-friendly tone, then he stepped down to congratulate them with a gentle handshake.

"May you have all the happiness in the world...huh... and of course... Who has the Merchant, has the world, am I right?" the Red King joked subtly then turned back to his throne, "Tonight my friends, we celebrate, the Red Castle will rejoice this spectacular moment, I, invite you to a Royal dinner banquet in celebration of your marriage," the Red King said.

"Thank you, your Highness," said the Merchant.

"I hope you keep this marriage unscratched and never lose it, for the loss of love is a man's loss of all," said the Red King with a noticeable hint of sadness in his voice, but he quickly snapped out of it. "Come on, go back to your ship. Have some rest, and I'll see you tonight," the Red King added.

"Right after the presents, your Highness, the men are about to..." The Red King quickly interrupted the Merchant's sentence.

"No! Today I shall receive no presents from you, Merchant. Tonight, I give you my present instead," said the Red King.

"Thank you for such generosity, your Highness," the Merchant nodded, then left the Royal Hall with Isabella.

The Red King gazed at them as they walked out...he stared at them.

)))

Chapter 45

After greeting the Red King, the Merchant took Isabella to the Silver Kingdom, greeted the Silver King, and then returned to his ship. His greetings this time were short and brief. It was clear that the Merchant was eager to spend more and more time with Isabella alone.

The first man waited for the Merchant aboard Venus and rushed to him as soon as he was spotted.

"Welcome back," the First Man greeted the Merchant.

"Thank you," said the Merchant, then looked to Isabella and the First Man again.

The First Man realised his misconduct and quickly greeted Isabella too,

"Welcome back, and congratulations. I heard that the wedding was exquisite."

"Thank you very much," answered Isabella with a complimentary smile.

"Is everything ok?" asked the Merchant, "you seem... different!" he added

"No, not at all...everything is fine. I am fine! Just wanted to tell you that the Mute has been cured and...uh... the spears and arrows are buried in the sand already as you instructed Merchant," said the First Man pretending to be comfortable.

"Ok," said the Merchant, then headed to the house.

After walking a couple of steps away, the Merchant stopped, looked back at the First Man, and asked, "Are you sure you are, ok?"

"Yes! Yes, I am," answered the First Man confidently with a mere smile,

The Merchant gazed at him for a second, then headed off.

)))

Chapter 46

That night at the Red Castle, a huge dinner table was set, a very long one right in the middle of the Red Castle's royal hall, music played, dancers swirled, and entertainers of all sorts left no space for a pinch of boredom, it was an exquisite royal dinner banquet. The Red King sat at the head of the table; the Queen sat opposite him on the other end. The Merchant and Isabella sat next to each other at the middle of the table, on the Red King's right and the Queen's left.

"Help yourself to more, feast," said the Red King to Isabella.

"Thank you, your Highness, but I am full...that is quite a feast, if I may say," said Isabella, setting her plate aside.

The Queen seemed gloomy and quiet. The Red King, of course, showed no concern. On the contrary, he was still overly friendly.

"Then let's have a drink to mark the occasion," the Red King said, signalling the servant to pour wine for the Merchant and Isabella.

"Pardon me, Red King, you know I don't drink," said the Merchant, "Well, this is something I always wondered about; how could a sailor not drink? Don't you wine down your water to keep your water fresh? Wine prevents it from going bad during months in the middle of the sea, am I right?" asked the King, "Yes, you are right. Wine does keep the water fresh, but so does silver; we use pure silver coins to keep our water and minds fresh at all times."

"Ah, an answer to every question and a new trick to every old way. No wonder everyone I know is fascinated by the Merchant," said the Red King, who seemed to be getting a little tipsy.

"May I ask you, and I have never asked you any...to have a drink with me tonight? After all, that is one occasion to celebrate," the Red King insisted.

Reluctantly the Merchant held the cup, and the servants filled it with wine. The Merchant looked at Isabella, smiling, and then he drank the wine. The Red King smiled and sat back on his chair "tell us, Isabella, how did you both meet? I bet it is an interesting story. Come on, tell us, don't be shy," said the Red King. Isabella smiled, "Nothing to be shy of, your Highness. I will tell you how we met."

Isabella held the Merchant's hand and started telling the story of how they first met. Her eyes were full of love and admiration whenever she looked at the Merchant. She took a deep breath; she seemed touched at heart to recall and tell their love story.

"I was walking in the woods, just about dusk, going home," Isabella said.

"She was wearing a red hood, carrying a breadbasket in her right hand," said the Merchant. Then Isabella continued, "Then I heard a sound, just as it got darker, I rushed my steps towards the cottage, I was scared, I rushed, but the sound was catching up with me, no matter how I sped up my steps, it caught up with me."

"What sound?" the Queen asked, with a sarcastic yet hidden tune, implying that Isabella was exaggerating facts, but the Red King cut her off.

"Let her finish her story, their story, let us know how they met in exact detail, " he cued Isabella, who felt a little uncomfortable. The Red King wanted Isabella to continue telling the story, so he cut the brief silence and said to her, "Please, go on!"

"As I said, I was afraid, it was dark, and the sound of something moving in the woods was catching up, so I started running. All I thought about was that I wanted to get home and be safe. I wasn't even curious to know what was making that sound. Anything or anyone following me in the woods at that time is something I'd rather not face.

I ran and ran; it got closer and louder. I looked behind, foolishly I tripped and fell to the ground, and there it was, its eyes, its steaming breath, a wolf, it was a wolf, a big strong, hungry and angry wolf. I thought that was it, I screamed, but before the wolf attacked me, he jumped in, out of the trees, at lightning speed, face to face with the wolf, holding two daggers in his hands. Before I knew it, they were rumbling around. He managed to climb on the wolf's back, and blood splashed out the second he did. He stabbed both daggers in the wolf's neck, one under each ear. The wolf fell, and the Merchant stood up," said Isabella as she looked at the Merchant with love.

"She stayed on the ground. She was so scared, I lent her my hand, but it took her a moment before she let me help her up," said the Merchant.

"He seemed to be so fearless that I feared him myself. I remember our conversation that night as he walked me home. I was overwhelmed by his bravery, so I asked him what he feared the most. I still remember the answer so clearly," Isabella said.

"So, what does the Merchant fear the most? That is such an interesting question. What does a man who travels the world and conquers all seas fear? What do you fear the most, Merchant?" asked the Red King.

"He told me that the only thing he feared was..." said Isabella before the Merchant interrupted her with the answer.

"Myself, I fear myself the most...your Highness...I fear myself the most,"

The Merchant rubbed his eyes; his vision suddenly seemed to blur.

"Don't tell that one cup of wine got to you, Merchant," said the Red King in a less friendly tone.

"Are you all right?" asked Isabella with concern.

"Yes, dear, don't worry, I am fine," answered the Merchant.

"So then, before the night comes to an early end, may I give you my present, my surprise for tonight," said the Red King as he got off his chair and started circling the table.

"Well, to be honest, and humble...that was a hard one, difficult even for a King. What would I get the Merchant as a wedding gift? After all, he has or can have anything he wants from any place around the world. How can I impress the Merchant with a single present, I thought to myself, and then it occurred to me, it must be artistic, art is the finest gift of all; And I am a writer, yes! I write poetry that no one knows about...words are the best gift I can present you."

The Merchant seemed increasingly off balance; he reached for the water and started gulping it all at once. However, the Red King continued, "So, I searched and searched my poems; lucky enough, I came across a better writer than myself. A writer who falls short of none when it comes to the expression of the emotions of love and passion. A great poem, but the writer didn't title the piece, so I entitled it myself to choose...I called it 'Ink & Blood'. Fury tore the Red King's smile as he pulled out of his pocket the Queen's wrinkled love letter to the Merchant and threw it into the middle of the table. The Merchant recognised the letter at once, and it was one of many he returned to her. The Queen gazed in shock. The Merchant, sweating and panting, was sure it wasn't just wine. The Red King poisoned him in revenge for the Queen's love for him.

"What is going on?" Isabella said in worry, "What is happening to you?" she cried out now that the Merchant could hardly speak.

"Guards," shouted the Red King as the music stopped, and everyone ran out of the hall. Many royal guards surrounded Isabella and pulled the Merchant away from her. The Royal guards held him in front of the Red King, and the Merchant was now too weak to stand. The Red King stepped closer to the Merchant and grabbed him close.

"We are almost even now," said the Red King to the Merchant. "You captured my Queen's heart, but I have captured your Isabella."

"I...I...I never...loved her back, " said the Merchant with short breaths.

"Oh, Merchant! Does it matter?" the Red King mocked him, then pulled out his dagger and stabbed the Merchant in his abdomen. Isabella cried out, and so did the Queen, "No!" The Red King pressed the blade in and whispered to the Merchant, "Go back to your fleet, order them to surrender without a fight, and if one does fire a single cannon at this castle, you'll never see Isabella again. I will slit her throat myself with this very dagger," then he pulled it out, and the Merchant screamed in pain, falling to the floor." The guards took Isabella out of the royal Hall by force, and the Queen ran to her chamber while the Red King stood atop the Merchant, who was still trying to gather his strength, despite the poison and his bleeding wound. "She was my world, and you stole her from me. Give me your fleet in return. Give me the world," said the Red King in bitter vengeance.

"No!" shouted the Merchant in a moment of strength, which drove the last bit of sanity out of the Red King's mind. So, he kicked the Merchant in the face and drew his sword, hitting and cutting the Merchant all over his body.

At that point, the First Man stormed in and stopped the Red King by blocking his sword and pushing him back. "What are you doing? If he dies here, they will flatten this whole castle to the ground. I said wound him, just wound him," the First Man yelled. The Red King sat on the ground, breathing heavily, and started to cry madly, lying on the ground. The Merchant couldn't believe what he heard and saw. A short moment later, the Merchant lost consciousness because of his wounds and shut his eyes.

Chapter 47

The First Man took the wounded Merchant back to the ship. He explained to the crew how the Red King had gone mad, captured Isabella in trade of the whole fleet, and wounded the Merchant. The First Man explained it all, not out of honesty, but instead, he acted according to the plan.

As soon as the Silvers heard about the incident, they sent their naval commander right away to Venus that night. The naval commander saw the Merchant lying with his wounds, bleeding and unconscious. The First Man tried many medicines, but nothing was enough to seal all those wounds and stop the bleeding. However, it did slow the bleeding down, yet it couldn't stop it. As much as the naval commander was concerned about the Merchant's well-being, he was also worried about what would happen next. If the Red King got hold of the Merchant's fleet, it only meant one thing to the Silvers...a wipeout of the silver fleet and later the whole Silver Kingdom.

"How is he doing?" the naval commander asked the First Man.

"Passed out, can't seal his wounds," answered the First Man.

"I will assemble every fighting ship we have and join your fleet to enforce it against any possible attacks," said the naval commander.

"The Merchant's men are capable of defending the fleet," the First Man stated.

"But the Merchant is wounded. Your men are concerned about their leader and will not fight with high morale. You need us... and we must defend the Merchant's fleet," the naval commander insisted.

"But won't you be stepping in the Red Kingdom's waters?" the First Man pointed out.

"Yes," nodded the naval commander.

"Well, that would make the standoff worse!" said the First Man.

"It already is," answered the naval commander. Then left the main deck back to the commanding ship.

The First Man knew that all he had to do now was wait because everything was going according to the plan...the well-laid plan.

Chapter 48

The Red King stood by the narrow window until dawn, gazing outside in silence. He seemed distant. Leaning one hand on the wall right above his head, the other hand clenched hard on the wrinkled love letter... the Queen's love letter to the Merchant. The Minister entered and seemingly needed to speak to the Red King.

"Sire!" the Minister called and waited for the Red King's reply, but he realised that the Red King didn't notice him, so he repeatedly called for his attention.

"Your Highness...Sire...my King!" the Minister spoke out a little louder,

"Huh!" the Red King finally noticed.

"I was wondering if the guards should..." the Minister managed to say before the Red King interrupted him.

"Keep your chin up," said the Red King.

"My King?" exclaimed the Minister.

"Keep your chin up, my father told me. Keep your chin up, his father told him. Keep your chin up, for a crown only falls off a lowered head," said the Red King, still gazing outside the window.

"Sire?" the Minister didn't understand the point. The Red King turned and commanded royally, "Declare Royal Anger."

"Pardon!" said the Minister with a trembling voice.

"Declare, Royal Anger", stressed the Red King with

every word.

"Sire... 'Royal Anger' is just...it has never been..."

"Declare Royal Anger," the Red King shouted his madness out, "Declare Royal Anger and condemn the Queen," the Minister stood still in shock. Tears filled the Minister's eyes, "But your Highness, Prima, my only daughter...Pardon her... let her go home before you declare..."

Here the Red King started the declaration himself,

"I... the King of the Red Kingdom myself...."

"No," pleaded the Minister.

"Declares Royal Anger upon the Red Marbled Castle..."

"No, your Highness, I beg you...pardon Prima, pardon Prima."

The Red King continued, "In condemnation of the Queen and ALL of her subjects." Then the Red King's hand clinched the Queen's love letter to the Merchant "Guards."

"Yes, our King."

"You may announce."

The Royal guards stomped their spears, loudly repeating the Red King's declaration, one after the other, from the castle's centre throne hall to the deepest hollow below. The Minister knew what it meant...he cried out, pulled his dagger, and jumped to stab the Red King in the back, but the Royal guards' spears were quicker than the Minister's sprint; their spears went through his stomach and out of his back.

The Red King turned and looked the Minister in the eye, coldly...until he dropped dead, spilling tears and blood while the hallows of the Red Castle echoed.

"Royal Anger...Royal Anger...Royal Anger."

Chapter 49

The Silvers assembled their fleet into several units. Most units were commanded to join and reinforce the Merchant's fleet, and a couple of units headed north. They were stationed there to give an early alarm and defend the northern front of the Silver Kingdom. They were stationed northeast.

As soon as they dropped anchor, men atop the main tower checked the horizon with their telescopes, a routine they were well trained for; they opened the telescope, starting from the east side, panned slowly to the west, then back to the middle of the horizon, to the furthest point up north. One after one, they all flawlessly performed the task.

"Oh my!" said one of the men as he looked deep into the northern horizon. By instinct, he put down his telescope, checked the horizon with his eyes, and then looked back through the telescope. Now he was sure of what he saw. A fleet, a whole fleet of pirate ships, not one or two, not a dozen or more, looked like all the pirate ships. Every pirate ship of all the seas had shown up as one.

He laid his telescope down, grabbed the horn hanging next to him, filled his lungs with all the air they could hold, and blew the horn.

Seconds later, one ship after another in the Silver naval unit blew their horns out loud, blew in warning of an imminent attack.

Chapter 50

Cannons atop the Red Castle fired shots of black smoke, one after another, the flags were dropped to half mast, and a big black flag was raised. A cloud of black smoke billowed above the castle after all the cannon shots.

Deep down in the darkest ends of the castle, dungeons opened. Dungeons that kept inside the Royal Anger executors were tall, broad, tough African men known for their lethal force. They had lived and trained in the dungeons every day and night for years. Being a Royal Anger executer was closer to a ceremonial position for 'Royal Anger' had never been executed, ever, the idea of its very existence was symbolic and strategic, but on that day, the dungeons were opened, masked, strong, big, bodied men in black leather and spikes were out to execute their task. They knew precisely what to do. They were called the Slayers.

Chapter 51

The First Man stood aboard Venus on the port side. The Silver naval commander stood next to him, and they gazed at the giant cloud of black smoke billowing over the Red Castle.

"What's that?" asked the First Man in concern.

The naval commander frowned as he knew what it meant, "That is something I knew but thought I'd never see...this...it can't be!" he abruptly said, almost mumbling.

"What does it mean?" exclaimed the First Man once again.

"It means that the Red King is angry to the extent that he's lost his mind. Anger made him mad; the Red King is angry like no other King has ever been...." The naval commander was interrupted by horns blowing on the horizon. He turned sharply to the north.

"What is that now?" asked the First Man.

The naval commander turned to the First Man and said, "Now you gather your ships and follow mine, 'now' is battle."

Chapter 52

A group of fair girls in white silk dresses ran across the halls of the Red Castle. Each one held a bucket full of black paint that looked very close to tar, black and thick. They swiftly spread across the halls, each girl at a painting of the Queen's face, any painting that had the Queen's face in it, a portrait or with the Red King or even in a group. They stopped at each painting and painted the Queen's face with black paint, covered her, ruined the paintings with black paint and that they let it drip, like tears, black tears of Royal Anger.

The Slayers went after the Queen's guards, slaughtering them mercilessly, whipping them, cutting off their limbs; screams of pain and panic were louder than the cling of sparking swords. The guards couldn't face the might of the Royal Anger's Slayers; they fell in pain one after one. The girls swept into the Red King's throne hall, turned the throne chair round, and started painting it black; they wheeled in a big crystal heart full of black paint and handed the Red King a small black metal hammer. The Red King broke the heart, set the hammer aside, dipped his hand into the black paint and took out a key.

The girls took the key from the Red King, ran to a black wooden door, and unlocked it. Behind the door lay a crown, seal rings, a sceptre, and a robe, all of which was a replica of the King's royal belongings, exact except, for one thing, they were all black.

They took off the Red King's crown and replaced it with a black replica; they took off his robe, laid a black one on his shoulder, and finally handed him the sceptre, the black sceptre. Throughout the process, the Red King kept his hand clenched on the Queen's love letter to the Merchant.

The screams of the Queen's guards at her chamber's doorstep were frightening. All maids sat on the floor in a stacked circle; they were crying and panicking with every scream of pain they heard, while the Queen sat on her throne, with her crown on; all dressed in white, the screams were frightening, yes, but not as frightening as the silence that followed.

The Queen knew that the Slayers had killed all her guards.

The maids screamed and held on to each other as the door banged and rattled.

The Queen trembled; the Slayers were tearing her chamber's door down. With every bang, the Queen trembled more, and the maids screamed their tears out and held on stronger to each other.

Not too many bangs later, the door shattered, it just fell off, and Slayers as big as the door itself stepped in.

The maids cried in silence and grabbed each other until their nails bled. The biggest Slayer walked in with slow, terrifying steps towards the Queen.

She tried to control her trembling as much as she could. She kept her crown on and her chin up.

The Slayer stood before her and then slapped the crown off her head.

The fair girls dressed in white silk entered in quick steps and headed right to the Queen's bathtub. They stood in two lines on both sides of the tub. They lifted their black paint buckets and rested them on their shoulders, holding the buckets with both hands and standing still.

After slapping off her crown, the Slayer pointed to the bathtub. The Queen stood up and walked slowly towards the tub in pride and pain. As she passed by her maids, she slid her hand over their heads, and as she did, they cried out loud, and she couldn't help dropping a tear herself. The Queen walked towards the bathtub; she stood atop it, at the stairs, and looked at the tub, full of creamy white water. Still trying to hold her tears and hide her trembling fear, she lifted her chin and looked at the Slayer.

The giant masked Slayer nodded to the girls, who instantly tilted the black paint out of the buckets. The Queen stepped down the stairs as the black paint splashed into the creamy white waters, gradually turning it black.

The Queen dipped in slowly to show pride but couldn't hold back her tears any longer as she saw her maids being snatched one after the other by the Slayers. Finally, she closed her eyes and dipped her head chin up into the thick black paint the fair girls kept pouring till the last drop. The Queen came back up, stepped up the stairs, painted in black from head to toe, stepped out, stood in front of the Slayer in submission and stretched her arms. The Slayer cuffed her in a thick heavy black chain and pulled her through the hall barefooted. The Queen stepped over bodies and slipped on warm blood. She tried not to look but couldn't; she looked at the bodies, the blood, and the black paint that covered almost everything she laid her eyes upon. Her knees grew weaker as they approached the Red King's throne hall; the Slayer opened the door, pulled her in to stand alone in front of the Red King, and face his Royal Anger.

Chapter 53

The Red King sat on his throne, now painted in black. The Queen saw his right-hand hanging, painted in black. She looked at the painting she was in; her face was painted black. The Red King held up his hand, holding her love letter to the Merchant and said one word, out loud, just one word.

"Why?" The Queen couldn't answer.

"Why?" the Red King shouted, clenching his fist on the letter. The Queen's silence provoked the Red King's anger, who then took an angered stride at the Queen and shouted in her face, "Why? you tell me why?" then he turned down in sadness. "What have I done to deserve this? After all, I've done...this!"

Then he shouted out again. "This is how you pay me back?" throwing the letter in her face. The Queen gathered her strength out of provocation and shouted back at him, "Pay you? Pay you back? What? Because you paid me! And what did you pay for in the first place? Me? Did you think you could buy me with all the pearls, silk and jewels you've given me? Or rather paid me! And you expected me to pay you back? No! All your trials to buy me didn't work."

"Buy you?" exclaimed the Red King.

"Yes...you thought you could..." the Queen argued.

"Buy you?" the Red King interrupted her again.

"Why are you...."

"Buy you! Buy you!" the Red King snapped open a chest next to his throne and pulled out a pearl necklace, held it in the Queen's face with a tight fist,

"These...these reminded me of your smile, so I bought them for you..."

He threw it on the floor towards the Queen and then pulled out a silk cloth.

"And this, this is how your skin felt to me, so I bought it for you..."

The Red King threw it, too.

It slid on the red marbled floor until it reached the Queen's bare feet, then he grabbed a handful of jewels,

"And these...all of these are not a fraction of how precious you are to me."

He dropped the jewels, opened his fist, and looked down at the floor in sadness.

The Queen stood silent...

The Red King looked her in the eye and said, "A man does what he can to express his love, and you...you were loved by a King. No! No, I never tried to buy you, for a King never buys his Queen."

She looked touched and disappointed at the same time, for she had never glimpsed such emotions in the Red King's love for her. But now it was too late. She wished she had known earlier. What a pity, now it was too late.

The Red King turned his back to her and shouted,

"Guards! take her to the dungeons." He heard her chains clinking as she tried to reach him, so the Red King shouted louder, "Take her away NOW." The Royal Guards pulled the chain, and out she went...from the throne hall to the dungeons.

Chapter 54

The First Man joined the Silver naval commander, merged many battleships, and headed straight to the pirate's fleet. They were sailing at top speed to the rescue of the Silver Kingdom and the Merchant's fleet. The battle had to be won, and the pirates stopped in the middle of the sea, or the damage would be severe. The Silver naval commander kept his eyes on the horizon. The First Man kept looking backwards at the Red Castle, gazing at this big black cloud of smoke billowing over it. He was worried for Prima more than before.

"What is going on in the Red Castle?" he thought to himself, "No one mentioned such a thing while we were planning all this, not the Minister, not the Red King, not even Prima."

He couldn't help asking the Silver naval commander once again.

"I am just curious, but what did we see at the shore, the Red Castle, the black smoke and the black flags? What is that all about?" he asked.

"Later," answered the Silver naval commander.

"Draw your sword and be ready; we are getting close," the naval commander added.

The cannons sounded closer, they were close to the battle spot, and it was obvious that the battle was fierce.

"I think we should split," shouted the First Man while the

sounds of the ongoing battle got louder as they got closer.

"What? Split? Now? Why?" asked the naval commander as he fastened his belt and checked his sword.

"They outnumber us; we must distract their attack... you go support the remaining Silver ships. I will circle to draw their attention and then find a weak spot. I will do them much damage," said the First Man, and it sounded logical to the naval commander, but something didn't feel right. However, they were past the point of argument, very close to the battle, and some pirates' ships even started firing their cannons at them.

"Right," said the naval commander in a loud voice, "Meet me in the middle," he added. He instantly took off to his commanding ship and signalled his unit to split.

"Something just doesn't feel right," the naval commander thought.

About 500 ships of the Merchant's fleet circled the battle spot. The First Man commanded them all. They were close to the pirates' fleet but not too close to getting hit by cannon fire. At that point, the First Man shouted his command, "Line up," the commander of each ship repeated the order so that all ships followed, and so each ship adjusted its speed precisely to line up one after another until a long line of ships was formed.

"Aye, Aye, captain," shouted the commander of each ship up until it reached the First Man's ship, marking the completion of the command.

"The line is formed," said the First Man's second in

command. "Then fire," the First Man ordered.

"Fire," "Fire," "Fire," "Fire," "Fire." The ships fired their cannons, and the Merchant's fleet was famous for its powerful long-range cannons. One pirate ship after another was hit repeatedly until it was shattered into pieces, but one thing grabbed the second commander's attention. After the first couple of shots, the pirate ships never fired back; they just waited there like sitting ducks while they got shattered.

"Why aren't they firing back?" he asked the First Man.

"Why would they?" answered the First Man with a smirk.

"I know we are out of their range, but still, they didn't, they didn't even try to get close...its...it..." the second in command seemed to have trouble finishing his sentence. He had a severe stomachache, sweating, panting, and his face started to pale out of colour. The First Man didn't pay attention and said, "They will get close." The second in command gathered his strength and looked at the debris through his telescope; he seemed surprised. "There aren't any bodies?" he said, breathing heavily and hardly maintaining his balance.

"No, the ships were empty, or they left just right before we shot at them." At that moment, the second in command dropped his telescope, held onto the First Man's arms, and then dropped to his knees. He heard the rest of the crew aching and vomiting, all except the First Man, who stood still. He looked to the First Man in blame and said in pain, "Why?"

"Why? the First Man thought to himself, then thought more, "because I am in love with the most beautiful fairness I have ever seen, Prima, the one whom I'd do anything to be with. I would lose it all to win her. They say love makes a fool out of a man, but no, I am not fooling myself. I know what I've done. I betrayed, I betrayed you all. Then he saw it all in his mind. I dropped the poisoned silver coins into the water tanks. Thirst is at its most, right before battle, two silver coins stuck together with a black sticky poison that the Blacks have given me; as soon as it dissolves, it disappears, no colour, no smell, no taste, no chance of survival. It kills; it certainly kills. I've killed you all...for love gets the best out of a person...or the worst."

"Throw the rope, don't leave us in the locker, throw us the rope," the second in command pleaded, but the First Man stood still and watched him choke to his death. The First Man then took out of his pocket a black paper roll and burnt it, setting it on fire like a torch. Thick black smoke came out, and so did the pirates from behind the shattered and burnt decoy ships, just as planned. They were to board the Merchant's ships, and wear the poisoned men's clothes, then throw their bodies into the waters, and so they did, and now the First Man controls half of the Merchant's fleet with pirates in disguise; all was going well all was going according to plan.

"Love gets the best out of one, or the worst," the First Man thought, "I betrayed for you...My love."

Chapter 55

The Mute, not a 15-year-old kid, ran back to his home. His mother was sweeping the dust in front of the house with a shorthanded broom.

She noticed her son running toward her; she instantly left the broom and dropped to her knees with open arms. The Mute threw himself into her arms, sheltering tightly in her hug.

"My sweetest, what's wrong?" she said as the Mute cried his tears out; she gently pushed him away with her hands around his face, and then she signed-languaged her question.

"He is hurt," the Mute signed in answer, "Badly. He is wounded badly. Blood everywhere, the Merchant, the Merchant is badly wounded." Then he threw himself into his mother's hug. She patted him on the back as he cried. His twin brother stood in shock a couple of steps away; she looked at him, opened another arm for him, and ran into her hug—no need to explain or elaborate on how important the Merchant was to this small family.

The Mother and her two sons. The twins were born after their father's death. He was killed, in a battle of no return with the pirates far beyond the horizon, in the middle of the sea, he never had a chance to see them, and neither did they. She always remembered the day they were born, so clearly as if it was a week ago; she was in hard labour, in pain, sweating and screaming. she also was so emotional, and her emotions spiked as soon as she laid her eyes on her firstborn, her twins, the pain was unbearable, not physically but emotionally, loneliness narrowed her chest, clutched on her heart, and squeezed tears out of her eyes. She was alone, and she would have to raise the twins on her own. She was afraid, sad and anxious. What a waste to the beauty of the moment, but then, at the very exact moment, he stepped in, the Merchant himself in flesh and blood, stepped into her poor house and pledged to take good care of her and her twins. She smiled in tears and held on to this particular moment's gratitude. The Merchant, as always, kept his word, paid off her debts, and supported them with gold coins, clothes, medicines, and whatever they needed, but most important of all, he taught the Mute how to speak sign language. She would've never communicated with her dearest or gotten to know him or expressed her love if it wasn't for the Merchant. The Merchant, who is now wounded, bleeding, was now dying.

Chapter 56

The Silver naval commander was one of the best commanders of the Silver Kingdom, a master of many different battles, but this time, somehow...was different.

The pirates were fierce and confident, pulling in and out in a well-laid naval tactic. They even started tightening their grip around his ships, making him instantly wonder, "Where are you?" stressing every word in his mind as he wielded his sword with all his strength.

Not only was the gun battle fierce, but some pirates even managed to board some ships, including his commanding ship, forcing him into a face-to-face sword fight.

In a glimpse, he saw the masts of the First Man's fleet; he felt relieved that 500 ships of the Merchant's fleet were more than needed to win this battle.

Anytime now, the cannons would fire, and the pirates would sink, just as planned with the First Man, and yes, the guns fired, smoke clouded the air, bangs echoed loud, and the Silver naval commander almost smiled. Still, shockingly the cannons weren't firing at the pirate ships but rather at the Silver ships, sinking them as quickly as rocks to the bottom of the sea.

Distracted by what he saw, the pirates fighting him used the opportunity and jabbed the silver commander's chin hard. He lost consciousness right away...and fell to the floor.

Chapter 57

A forest was technically the Red Castle's backyard. Trees, fallen leaves and dark soil from the castle's back gate to the hills that overlooked everything, the Red Castle, the Silver Castle, the Crab Gulf, and the Teardrop Isles.

Atop that hill started another tree line for another forest. Just before that tree line, the naked part of that hill gave any observer a perfect panoramic view. It must be how maps were drawn those days; a black horse carriage stopped at that spot. It was the Blacks family's Dean.

He was known for keeping a close eye on what makes or breaks the family's future and kept that eye in person that day. He couldn't be away and wait for the results. He had to be there at that spot to witness the execution of his well-laid plan.

That day was the start of all days for him and his family. The Merchant, The Merchant's fleet and men, The Red Kingdom, and the Silver Kingdom will all fall tonight. They will burn in fires...fires that will light the way for the Black Family to rise.

Chapter 58

The Silvers were watching from the Kingdom's highest towers and saw everything. They saw the Merchant's men dying and thrown into the waters. They saw the pirates disguising in the Merchant's men's clothes to disguise. They saw the Silver naval Commander and his men slaughtered, the pirates taking over the ships, but worst of all, they saw the First Man's betrayal. They had witnessed his darkness.

"They are heading to us," said one Watcher to the other. "They will be here by night; hurry to the commanders," he said.

"Shall I send someone to warn the Merchant's fleet, too?" he asked.

"The commanders will tell us what to do. Hurry to them, now!" he stressed.

He rushed down the tower as ordered; while the Watcher returned to his telescope, he saw the Merchant's half fleet at the Crab Gulf and half the Silver's fleet at the docks, and he saw the pirates, sailing towards the shore, then thought to himself, "They are going to attack... tonight."

Chapter 59

Horns blared in the Silver Kingdom's air. Horns that most villagers had never heard in their lives. However, they all knew what it meant. Scared, tense, crying and panicking, villagers lined up in front of their houses. They knew the drill, gather your family and loved ones, carry only your most essential belongings, and wait in front of your house.

The Silver guards came to lead them out, out of the Kingdom. It was an evacuation because they were awaiting a major seaborne attack, and the Reds had lined up downhill for a land offence.

The Silver Kingdom was never in a more threatening attack from both sea and land.

It was a full offensive.

Chapter 60

The Line Guards was a familiar name in the Red Kingdom and the Silver Kingdom. They were the guards at the border line that separated the two neighbouring Kingdoms. There was no forest between them, no river, sea, mountain or any other of nature's border lines.

The Silver Kingdom topped a hill, and the Red Kingdom centred the lowlands. The borderline is where the Red Kingdom stopped, and the Silvers' hill went up to the highest point.

The Silvers had their guards at the gates and walls. Some other silver guards patrolled the hill but never crossed the line.

The line was always guarded by the Red Kingdom's Line Guards, who were strong, fierce, and charged to fight and kill at any moment.

The Line Guards stood fast, held, and walked the line, disciplined to their leaders, savage at fights. They had special weapons, special shields, special armour and exceptional leadership, highly trained and highly skilled.

The Saharan led them, a brutal, savage military man, strong beyond any man's force, skilled beyond anyone's training, and loyal, the most faithful to the Red King.

They say that the Red King rescued him from losing his life to thirst in the middle of the desert. An Arabian desert the Red King went to on one of his expeditions. Saving the Saharan was one of the few times the Red King showed kindness, or maybe an intelligent act by which he won himself a devoted, strong, and skilled soldier. Since then, the Saharan defended the line and was always ready to attack the Red King's enemies anytime and at any cost.

The Saharan lined up with his soldiers, and then more and more troops lined up with his soldiers, all on attack formation for the first time in their prolonged standoff.

The Reds were about to attack the Silvers.

Chapter 61

The Mute and his twin sat next to their mother in the caves they reached by nightfall.

For decades those caves had offered sanctuary for the Silver Kingdom's people. A well-protected place that the old, sick, and young hid in with their mothers, sisters, and daughters. They resorted to those during battles.

The young ones were terrified because this was their first time. There were many candles in the cave; the silver soldiers kept the sanctuary well equipped and ready for such emergencies.

The Mute's mother lit up one after another and started handing them out.

Elders and children wrapped themselves up with wool sheets seeking warmth and comfort. After the candles were lit and everyone held one, the Mute's mother started to sing a prayer, and they all joined her.

The twins held their candles and stared at their mother as she led the singing prayer. It was a moonless night, easy for warships to hide on the horizon, so the silver ships, or rather the remaining half of the Silver fleet, stood their defence formation a little offshore, waiting for their enemy to approach under the dark curtain of a moonless night.

They had learnt that defence was the best strategy to be followed on such nights. They waited, but no ships showed up so far; it was a silent and chilling night. The waters were too calm, troubling. Everything felt troubling, especially the waiting.

Chapter 62

The Merchant laid on his bed, wounded, unconscious, breathing slowly, or every couple of seconds, not breathing at all.

His men stood around him, sad and confused, for they had never seen their master helpless. They had never been in a situation with him that felt hopeless. The healers couldn't stop the slow bleeding. He was cut all over his chest, stomach, and shoulders. His teeth were covered with blood, and his bed sheets were all blood wet. It was a sad moment. They all felt desperate for the first time.

A healer sat on the edge of the bed, his eyes full of un-dropped tears and his heart filled with unbearable heaviness.

"Master!" he called gently as he passed a small bottle under the Merchant's nose, "Merchant...Merchant," he called out loud and almost broke into tears, but the Merchant remained unconscious.

At that moment, the room's door slammed open, and the packed crowd made way for Ji Kai. Naturally, they all stepped back, out of his way as he entered the Merchant's room and approached the bed where the Merchant lay half alive.

The healer stood up and stepped away. No one was sure if Ji Kai came to bid farewell to his Master or came to help revive him.

They all found it a bit possible that the old man had one particular trick left that could save the Merchant's life. They all hoped so.

'Ji Kai' pulled his hand out of his pocket, holding a small bottle filled with a noticeably glowing blue liquid. He opened the bottle and slowly filled the Merchant's wounds with it. The liquid was still glowing. 'Ji Kai' then put some liquid in his hand and brushed the Merchant's teeth. He emptied the bottle and stood still for a moment, with everyone around him anticipating a move. Suddenly, the Merchant inhaled a deep breath.

Ji Kai circled his hand over the Merchant's chest; the Merchant arched his back and inhaled so deeply with every move of Ji Kai's hand. His eyes were closed, but still, he responded to Ji Kai. The Merchant almost lifted his back off the bed, but suddenly, he dropped back, exhaling a long breath.

A few seconds turned to a couple of minutes, yet the Merchant lay still. He did not inhale. He did not move. He did not breathe. At that moment, Ji Kai started to wave his hands in circles over the Merchant's head and body, mumbling words or sounds that no one understood, but everyone felt it. It was sad. It all sounded sad.

Ji Kai stretched his arm under the Merchant's shoulders and knees, then surprisingly lifted him off the bed.

He carried the Merchant all alone, despite his old age. He walked out of the room carrying the Merchant. Everyone made way again but followed him with heavy steps.

Ji Kai walked on deck until he reached the plank at the ship's port side.

He walked to the plank's edge, closed his eyes, took a deep breath, looked up to the sky, and then rolled the Merchant off his arms. He dropped him into the sea as accustomed to their funerals.

The Merchant dropped like a rock to the seabed, leaving behind a cloudy trail of blood.

Ji Kai threw a rope into the waters, the spirit rope, for the Merchant's spirit to climb back up to the ship. At that moment, they were all sure that the Merchant was gone.

Ji Kai started chanting in some language, over and over, winds began to blow, lighting and thunderstruck in the skies, and it started to rain, waves splashed. Ji Kai dropped more of the blue bottles he had into the waters, and then it began to bubble rapidly as if boiling. Sharks circled the spot, driven in by the Merchant's blood. Ji Kai chanted louder, the waters rambled, and the winds blew stronger.

Suddenly, the loose rope tightened, they looked to see what was pulling the rope, and they saw a hand stretching out of the water and holding onto the rope. Yes, it was him. It was the Merchant. He pulled himself out of the rumbling waters and circling sharks. As thunderstruck louder, he pulled himself back to the ship, back to his ship.

He climbed up and stood in front of Ji Kai. The Merchant was panting, his veins pumped up, his wounds filled up and sealed with that glowing blue liquid, and his eyes looked sharp and focused. Ji Kai rumbled his enchantments, dipped his thumb into more of the glowing blue liquid, and then marked the Merchant's forehead with it.

The Merchant jammed his way in steady steps through his cheering men, then ran to the main mast and climbed to the top. He moved lightly and quickly all the way up. When his men saw him climb, all the mast men ran to their ships and climbed too.

When the Merchant reached the top, he grabbed a red horn and blew it out loud, each ship blew its red horn in turn, and by the time all the horns were blown out, PaleFace loaded three big cannons with as much gunpowder as they could take, only gunpowder, no cannon balls, he filled them up to the core and fired three guns one after another. They were so loud that the Queen trembled with the first shot fired. It shook the dungeon deep in the Red Castle.

The Red King drew his sword as he heard and was shaken by the second shot. The Merchant, up the mast, roared a yell as PaleFace fired the third shot, everyone heard the shots, and everyone knew what it meant. The Merchant was back, and the Merchant was ready to fight.

Chapter 63

The First Man heard the horns, heard the cannons boom three times.

"Stop here! Drop the anchors," he commanded loudly.

"What? Why?" asked one of the pirates.

"Haven't you heard? The horns and the cannons? The Merchant is back. He was almost dead. Now he is back," the First Man explained nervously.

"So?" the pirate shook his shoulders.

"So! Aren't you aware of whom we are dealing with, of whom we have rivalled? You might think it is all about the ships and the fleet but trust me, because I was his right hand and First Man, none of you would want to face the Merchant now.

We anchor here tonight and wait," the First Man insisted.

"Wait for what?" exclaimed the pirate.

The First Man turned and said, "For the Merchant to attack the Red King."

Chapter 64

It was dawn. It was cold, silent, and misty. The Red soldiers lined up ashore in full armour and sharp spears. They stood silent and ready for the unknown.

No one could see what was coming next. They all stared at Venus from where the Merchant would make his move.

The Merchant sat on the edge of his bed, gazing out the window into the pale first light of day. He grabbed a little crystal bottle full of the blue liquid, opened it, and then started slowly pouring and rubbing it all over his head and body.

All the Merchant's crew changed their clothes, sailors, cooks, and healers. Everyone changed into one costume, the war costume. It was coloured in gold, white and red. They are now fighters, warriors and defenders of the Merchant, Venus, and the fleet. They all lined up aboard their ships.

A large cymbal, a tam-tam gong, was placed atop the Merchant's house. The fleet's gong master banged the gong with a wrapped mallet. A terrifying sound rose to the sky in an intimidating crescendo. The Red soldiers had never heard anything like it before, but it was closest to the sound of thunder and racing heartbeats.

The Merchant came out of the house, and as soon as he did, soldiers on deck started to beat their drums. Everyone looked toward Venus. The Reds, the Silvers, the Blacks, the pirates, and those behind walls. The Merchant's men then lowered a small boat into the water, and the Merchant descended to it on a rope. As he stepped onto the boat, the six men onboard started rowing towards the shore. The Merchant stood at the bow with his eyes focused on the Red Castle and kept his balance all the way to shore.

The Red soldiers' heartbeat was in their throats as they saw the Merchant nearing, and they all thought, "The Red King couldn't kill the Merchant. The Merchant healed his wounds. He is strong and angry, and he is coming to us." They were terrified, but even more terrifying was that the Beasts, down in the dungeons, started roaring, higher and higher, as the Merchant got closer and closer.

The Red King watched it all from behind a narrow window in the throne hall, and as soon as he saw the Merchant approach shore, he called on his guards, "Get Isabella here now!"

The Merchant stepped off the boat while his men held it steady from each side, standing in water up to their knees. The Merchant looked up to the Red Castle's narrow windows. Isabella could be anywhere inside. Re-living the moment Isabella was taken from him made his blood boil in his veins. He went into the Red Castle alone in a rushing, steady step.

For the first time, the Merchant walked through the hallows of the Red Castle unannounced. Royal Anger's protocol doesn't welcome anyone.

The royal guards pinned their backs to the walls as the

Merchant passed through. When he reached the throne hall, the doors opened slowly. The Merchant saw the Red King standing next to the now black-coloured throne, and at the furthest corner stood a strong guard holding Isabella and pressing a sharp blade to her neck.

With a piercing look, the Merchant took a black wooden box out of his pocket and threw it to the Red King.

"Is that the key?" asked the Red King as he caught up the box and looked the Merchant back in the eye.

"Yes," answered the Merchant. The Red King turned the box up and round, trying to figure out how to open it; it seemed to be a solid piece of wood.

"How does it open? It has no key holes, no knobs!" asked the Red King.

"Burn it," the Merchant answered.

"What?" exclaimed the Red King.

"The box is a solid piece of wood, but the key is inside it, and it is metal; burn it, burn the wood and get the key out of the ashes," the Merchant said.

"The more precious the savings are, the trickier the safe gets," said the Red King, then snapped his fingers. A guard next to a torch promptly took it off the wall and handed it to the Red King.

Slowly and carefully, the Red King burned a corner of the wooden box with the flaming torch. The corner tip caught fire quickly but burnt slowly, fuming up a thin thread of black smoke.

"But how would I be sure what is inside is the actual

key?" the Red King asked.

"It changes colour in the rain. The key turns from sky blue to purple if exposed to raindrops," the Merchant answered.

"Well, look," the Red King pointed out the narrow windows, "It is not raining. I don't see, hear, or smell any rain. I then just have to drown Venus to know." Then he began to raise his voice, "I must make sure that you didn't just give me a false key. That would be horrible. You have to stay here, you and her, in the Red Castle, down in the dungeons until I drown that bloody ship and open the safe with that key you say is the right one."

At that moment, the fires started to burn through the wooden box rapidly, the smoke got thicker and thicker, and the fires whizzed rapidly through the black box.

The Red King instantly threw it away. It dropped in the middle of the throne hall, spun, and exploded!

The thick black smoke quickly filled up the hall. Everyone fell to the ground in shock. Their ears rang while swords started clanking outside. After the brief shock, everyone inside started coughing hard except for the Merchant, who instantly jumped on the guards next to him and snapped their necks with his bare hands. Outside the throne hall, the guards couldn't see through the smoke screen; for a moment, they were cautiously hesitant to enter. The Merchant knew that time was very tight. He had to reach Isabella. He could hear her coughing across the hall. Meanwhile, the thick black smoke billowed out of the narrow windows, and PaleFace directed Venus' cannons towards the smoking window.

Quickly the Merchant leapt across the hall. The Red King, the guards and Isabella were all on the floor coughing hard. He reached Isabella and dropped a few droplets into her mouth. She instantly stopped coughing and took a deep relieving breath in. He looked around and found the shadows of the Red King and guards on the floor, coughing and turning. He also saw the shadows of more red guards stepping into the throne hall. Quickly, he held Isabella and tucked her in a corner; just a second later, Venus' cannon boomed, firing directly at the throne hall's outer wall, opening a huge hole and tearing down the tower next to it into rubble.

The Merchant grabbed Isabella and slid on the rubble out of the throne hall and out of the Red Castle's walls.

Chapter 65

The Saharan found it an excellent opportunity to use the distraction the bombing caused and advance uphill to attack the Silvers.

"Follow me," he said to his troops, then swiftly crossed the line.

The Saharan knew that he only had a moment of distraction, and he used that moment well to sneak uphill with his troops, but here the Silver Arch Knight alerted and commanded the archers, "Attack."

Bows were shot. Spears were thrown, and the silver troops rained down on the Line Guards. It was a fierce defence, but the Saharan used the terrain to his advantage and hid behind the rocks. As soon as the Silver Archers stopped to reload, the Saharan led his troops a little more up and hid quickly behind the rocks before the other wave of arrows and spears rained down. He was advancing slowly, but he was advancing smartly and steadily.

Chapter 66

The Merchant and Isabella were circled by the Red Guards as soon as they slid down the rubble. Behind the Red Guards, the Merchant saw that three of his six men were killed, and the other three were fiercely sword fighting a huge number of red guards.

The cannons can't fire now, or they would kill them all. It was a man-to-man fight, and the Merchant was outnumbered onshore. Isabella hid behind his back, shaking and crying.

Suddenly, the Red Guards started to step back. The Merchant noticed that they were looking behind him, above his head. Isabella screamed, then froze in fear. The Merchant turned to find the two Beasts stepping from behind the rubble and dust the cannon fire brought down the walls of their cages too.

By instinct, the Red Guards froze too, but the Merchant didn't. He stepped closer to face the two Beasts while Isabella was frighteningly holding hard to his back. The Beasts circled slowly around the Merchant, roaring their sharp teeth out. They stepped closer to the Merchant and started sniffing slowly, rapidly, deeper and deeper. The Beasts' fur began secreting the same glowing blue liquid underneath their skin. At that moment, some of the Red Guards were sneaking slowly to surprise attack the Beasts and then kill the Merchant, but the two Beasts felt them stepping closer and roared everyone away. Then one beast closed its eyes and lowered its head at the Merchant's feet. The Merchant quickly grabbed Isabella and climbed onto the Beast.

As soon as the Merchant and Isabella mounted the Beast's back, it roared louder than any red soldier's courage, then ran towards the Teardrop Isles.

The other beast fought off all swords and spears until the Merchant and Isabella crossed the waters and rode into the thick trees of the isles.

The three remaining men of the Merchant's fleet fought fiercely and bravely and kept many Red soldiers off the Merchant's back, but they couldn't escape back to the fleet because there were too many Red soldiers. The brave six died ashore.

After the Merchant and Isabella got off the Red Castle's shore and the brave six down, PaleFace was cleared to bombard the Red Castle to the ground. But just before he ordered the gunners to fire the cannons, he heard the high mast sailor screaming, "Treason, treason."

PaleFace looked through one of the hatches with his telescope and saw what the high mast sailor saw on the horizon. He saw the pirate ships with half the Merchant's fleet sailing toward them. He saw their leader standing at the bow of their commanding ship. He saw the First Man, the traitor.

"Switch range, lock the floors and seal the Belly," PaleFace shouted his command. Instantly men on all fire floors rushed to execute the orders, all doors were sealed, and they switched the long-range cannons with the short-range ones, and the Belly was sealed to secure the gold it held.

"Fire," shouted PaleFace, the long-range cannons fired at the Pirates' ships, who kept on advancing and retreating, engaging and disengaging with the remaining battleships of the Silvers' and the Merchant's fleet that kept Venus' long-range cannons pointing to the sea line, just as the First Man planned. The Red Castle was relatively safe, and the red soldiers only had to face some fixed and stationed short, ranged cannons on their way to board Venus.

The Red soldiers streamed into the waters to board Venus. The short cannons fired one after another, but the red soldiers kept pouring. The guns slowed them down but didn't stop them. The Red soldiers knew that they had to seize Venus before the Merchant reached it, and they were succeeding.

The Dean smiled as he sipped his wine and watched it all from the hill.

Chapter 67

The Red King leaned his hands on the wall and stood up. He was still coughing lightly. The black smoke cleared out of the throne hall, and the injured and the dead Red Guards were carried out one after another. The throne hall was damaged. A massive hole in the middle of its wall bared it open to the seaside.

The Red King stood over the rubble and saw a pleasing scene. He saw the red soldiers climbing up Venus, fighting and taking control of the main deck, while the red soldiers on shore took down the Beast at the passage to the Teardrop Isles. Now the Red soldiers could cross the water and hunt down the Merchant. Now there was nowhere for him to escape.

As soon as the red soldiers took control of Venus' main deck, they rushed to the leveller, the main target set by the First Man. They circled it, and the strongest soldier among them pulled the leveller. They all heard the gears roll and cling, the cannons drew back from the hatches and all the hatches closed. The Red soldier rushed to the fire floor's doors, but they couldn't break them down; their axes broke the wooden layer of the doors but couldn't puncture through the alloy metal layer. They rushed to the Belly and faced the same metal doors beneath the wood. It can now only be opened by the key the Merchant had. The doors of the fire floors were sealed, but the red soldiers waited outside each one while PaleFace and his men were inside. The cannon hatches were closed and could only be opened from the main deck. PaleFace and his men were all locked in helplessly.

The First Man stopped manoeuvring and started advancing towards the Merchant's fleet to herd it under his command.

The pirates lined up their ships away from shore to draw the silver navy towards them and away from any ground support or chances to retreat and regroup.

The Saharan and his Line Guards kept the Silver Knights busily engaged in a series of attacks, draining out the silver defence and wasting their arrows and spears that would sooner or later run out.

The Silver Arch Knight was sure of the only way to survive this. It was obvious. "Sooner or later, the Saharan will reach the top. And who knows who would win then? The Saharan is a savage, and he fights like a one. Some say he could kill more than twenty men alone, but if we attack him on his way up, we will have the highland advantage over him, but if we wait, we could lose the Archers' Towers, the Silver Kingdom's only defence.

The Line Guards had to be stopped down there. The Silver Knights must now change their strategy and step into battle. It's time to face the Saharan and his Line Guards in a face-to-face survival battle.

The Silver Arch Knight drew his sword and shouted, "Line up for attack!"

Chapter 68

Cannons of the battling pirates' and the Silvers' ships echoed in the horizon's dome as the First Man stood proudly aboard Venus. Now it was under his control.

"Did you take the fire floors?" the First Man proudly asked a Red Soldier.

"No. We couldn't. The floors are sealed with steel doors just like the Belly," the red soldier answered.

"What?" the First Man seemed astonished. It was a well-kept secret the Merchant hid away from everyone except the gunners.

"Then stay at the doors and aboard. Sooner or later, we will have the key," said the First Man. Then he looked at the Red Castle's shore and was shocked to see the mess it and its shore were in.

His concern for Prima mounted rapidly. He scanned the whole shore with his eyes. Dead bodies of the red soldiers and the Merchant's men scattered on shore, blood-coloured the waters red; he saw the Red Castle almost split in half, black flags rose, the injured crawling, the Teardrop Isles be sieged by red soldiers at both ends. He grabbed his telescope and looked deeper into the now split-open Red Castle.

"Who are they?" he asked one of the red soldiers, pointing at the Royal Anger Slayers. "I've never seen those before!" he added.

"They are men of Royal Anger, the Red King declared Royal Anger, and they carried it out. The Slayers!" the red soldier answered.

"What Royal Anger? What Slayers?" the First Man asked in worry.

"The Red King ruined the castle, and the Slayers killed everyone in the royal court or threw them in the dungeons. He even killed the Minister when he tried to stop him," the red soldier sadly said.

"And Prima! Where is Prima." The First Man gripped the red soldier from his shield to shake an answer out of him. "Where is Prima?" he shouted.

"I don't know; only the royal guards are spared. She must be k...killed or in the dungeons!" the red soldier answered nervously.

The First Man let him go, turned to the pirates he had with him and commanded, "Ready three small boats, and pack them with your best men...we are going in, we are going to the Red Castle...now!"

Chapter 69

The Merchant made his way through the Teardrop Isles one after another. Some isles were close enough to be crossed from one isle to another. He rode the Beast with Isabella holding onto his back, crossing the narrow waterways one after another, from one isle to another. He wanted to reach the last isle to the open sea, the isle from which he could get to Venus.

He stopped the Beast and made it kneel. "Come on," he said to Isabella as he hopped to the ground, "Where are we going?" Isabella asked in such fragile self-control as she took his hand and stepped down the Beast.

"I will hide you," said the Merchant.

"What?" she almost snapped.

He instantly held her and explained, "I must sneak to the last isle and check it before we step on it. I don't hear any of my cannons firing. If my gunners didn't bombard the Red Castle must be because they couldn't. I am afraid Venus is taken."

"And what are we going to do then? Where would we go?" she cried lowly.

"We will get back on Venus. But I will have to go alone first. Trust me. I will hide you well, and I will not be late. There is no other way to do this. I must go and check."

Isabella nodded and held him tight.

Chapter 70

The First Man rowed the three boats slowly and carefully through the waterways between the Teardrop Isles. He wanted to go round the isles, reach an off-site point of the shore, sneak into the Red Castle, and then search for Prima.

He couldn't afford to waste time-fighting the Slayers at the shore or the gates. He would sneak in with his men. He knew how. He was good at it. He never got caught all those times he sneaked into the Red Castle to see Prima, his love.

They were rowing slowly not to cause any noise and, most importantly, not to confront the Merchant. The First Man fixed his eyes on the heavy trees and thick bushes as they passed near the isles. He knew that the Merchant was in there. He knew that if they crossed ways, they would fight, and though he had many pirates with him, he was a skilled fighter. Yet is still a great risk to fight the Merchant.

"Faster, row a little faster," he whispered.

Chapter 71

Deep in the Teardrop Isles, the Merchant hid Isabella up on the branches of a high tree.

Slowly and quietly, he sneaked a peek over the Beasts' back and saw the red soldiers lined up at the shore of the last Teardrop Isle, the one to the open sea, the closest isle to Venus. Though he had the Beast, he didn't plan to attack because he saw that Venus was seized and its cannon hatches closed.

He can't take them all out in a single attack, so he instantly planned in his head to wait and be more patient than them.

The Merchant planned to wait as long as it took and ambush them one by one as they came for him.

Chapter 72

The wait was unbearable to everyone in the caves. Everyone was tense, nervous, and afraid. Everyone sat tight, lost in deep thoughts and worry, except the Mute. He had his eyes fixed, staring at one person, one face, one girl.

He stared at a girl who sat quietly across the cave, a girl whom he had always loved.

He never knew her name, but he loved the way she looked. She had a long face, long neck, long hair, and a stunning clear smile. Yes, clear; he had always felt and seen clarity in her smile. She was untainted by the dust of poverty; her inner purity always preserved her beauty, and that was all he needed to know about her to fall in love with her. She was a couple of years older than him. He never dared to speak to her. The Mute was very confident in his wits and charm. However, that confidence never seemed enough to have pushed him her way. He never dared to express his feelings to her, but he had enough hope to dream. He always imagined how it would feel to be with her, in love, happy, intimate, the places they would go to, the laughs they would share, the gifts he would have given her. Dreams stuck in his imagination except one, a pearl, a gift he would have given her in real life; knowing that divers in the far east had to dive deep into the sea, holding their breath more than any man can, risking their lives, to get one of those; and he brought her the best one he could find. He bought it for her and kept it in his pocket for years, yet he couldn't gather enough courage to give it to her every day.

"What are you waiting for," he felt the thought, "This could be the last night of your life. Give her the pearl. Make it count."

He stood up and walked towards the group of orphans sitting together at the cave's end. She was an orphan herself, kind of their leader and caretaker.

The Mute stepped in, grabbed the pearl out of his pocket, all wrapped in soft orange cloth and just sat in front of her.

She gazed at him. He stretched his arm and opened his palm.

Chapter 73

The Red King sat on his throne, staring at the rubble through the wide cannon hole that had split open the Red Castle.

One of the commanding Red Guards entered the messed-up royal hall and addressed the Red King in a concerned voice, "Your Grace, The Merchant hasn't come out of the Teardrop Isles yet. What shall we do?"

"Did we get the gold?" the Red King asked.

"No, your Highness, the Belly is sealed in steel," the Red Guard answered.

"Did anyone get the key or at least know where it is?" the Red King asked again.

"No, your Grace," the Red Guard answered.

"Then send our soldiers in the isles to capture the Merchant. Capture him, and bring him to me after we get the key. I want to kill him myself," said the Red King.

"At your command, my King," the Red Guard stomped his feet and was about to turn and leave, but the Red King asked him, "And the Silvers! Have we taken them out yet?"

"No, your Grace, they are putting on a long fight. The Saharan is still trying to seize the Arched Towers, and the pirate ships are still engaging with the silver fleet at sea. They are keeping the Silvers away from Venus, yet they can't take them out and invade the shore to take the Silver Kingdom out," the Red Guard answered.

The Red King nodded. Then the Red Guard remembered

to add, "Your Grace, I will send in our men, but the Merchant still has the Beast with him. He rode it into the isles."

"Then send your men at dusk. Beasts are at their weakest at dusk."

"Would the Merchant hide in there that long?" exclaimed the Red Guard.

"I bet he will," said the Red King.

The Red Guard turned to leave, but the Red King had one last command before he left, "Send me my painter. I want him to paint me here on the throne, over that rubble."

Chapter 74

"It's almost nighttime. Why is it taking so long?" the girl sighed and asked the Mute. He couldn't hear her, but he understood her. She liked him; she liked the pearl he had given her. She had never had this kind of attention before. She felt like falling for him quickly. The rush was exciting for her.

Suddenly, a Silver Guard appeared at the cave's entrance. He looked weary, face bruised and dented shield, "Get ready to leave," he shouted.

They all cheered and felt relieved they were returning to their homes, but the Silver Guard shouted, "You are not going back to the village."

They all went so quiet.

"We can barely hold the shore; we can hardly resist the Saharan. Run! You should all run; the kingdom...the Silver Kingdom...is going down!"

Chapter 75

Down at the Red Castle, the First Man finally made it to the dungeons, three stories below, beneath the ground, away from sunlight, darkness rotting the walls, the floors, and the doors. Everything was painted in tar, black...all black, blackness that would cease any ray of light that comes astray.

There were few guards down there, and the pirates rushed, fighting and killing them. He stood still at the stairs, his feet grew cold, and fear took the best of his heart. Of course, not the fear of battle nor the awful site of the grave-like dungeons; instead, it was the fear of what he might find. "What if she's hurt? What if she'd...?" he couldn't even think of it.

With slow steps, he walked towards the dungeons; swords were clinging and sparking around him, and prisoners locked up there started rattling their chains rhythmically, yelling out in their weak voices, "Mercy, Mercy."

The First Man walked, passing those who yelled and those who pleaded. In slow steps, he walked until the end of the hollow. It was darker there, cold and suffocating. Something grabbed his attention, and he drew his feet towards it. He saw a well, a round stoned well. A well with no buckets and no ropes. He knew that the Red King got very creative in torturing his enemies. This well must be much worse than any of those dungeons.

"I will look there first," he thought.

If it is dry, then it must be soaked in blood. Blood of bodies thrown down there. He walked towards the well in slow steps. He grabbed a flaming torch to help him see what was on the darkest end of the hollow.

As he stepped closer to the well, he saw a heavy iron web capping the well with human limbs hanging out of its holes. Arms and legs were covered in blood, with the dead bodies piled and stacked down the dark well. One of the hands made him drop his torch as soon as he saw it. He instantly fell on his knees to the ground. One of the hands wore a ring, the ring that he had placed on her finger himself. One of the hands was Prima's.

"Oh, Prima," he cried. He held her hand. It was cold and blue; her hand had no life in it. He held her finger and kissed it gently; in tears and pain, he said, "Prima is dead! Oh, Prima! The blade must have been cold, oh my dear Prima, my sweet helpless Prima, they have cut you to death. You must have been scared. How couldn't he have any mercy on you? You were weak, your knees must have shaken, your stomach upset, your mouth dry, and your eyes shed tears. You must have looked your slayer in the eyes and silently begged him to spare your life. You must have trembled and shaken. You must have felt cold, Prima, and I couldn't take you in my arms and warm you up. You must have been so afraid and the pain. Oh, the pain you've felt! The blade must have been cold as it cut through your warm heart. Oh, dear Prima! I am sorry I wasn't there; I am sorry the blade must have been cold."

He sat on the ground next to the well, still holding her finger and crying with grief.

Chapter 76

Just as they were about to leave the caves, the Mute signed to his mother,

"Where will we go?"

"I don't know, but we have to run now," she signed back.

"It is stupid. We would be fooling ourselves if we thought we could make it out of the Silver Kingdom alive; even if we did, the Red Guards would hunt us down. The Red King has always wanted to wipe us out! And how far can we go? All the lands around the Kingdom are his. All the Kingdoms around are his!" the Mute signed.

"What's going on, come?" said one of the old men.

"My son is saying that we are doomed, and the Reds will kill us whether we stay in the caves or run," the Mute's mother answered.

"We've got to try," said the old man. "There is no other way; there is nothing else we can do!" he added.

"No, there is," signed the Mute, and his mother told the others.

"Hurry up, all of you back there," said the silver soldier.

"Wait a minute!" shouted the girl, or Pearl as the Mute now called her.

"There is one thing we can do to get out of this," here, the Mute's words grabbed everyone's attention as his mother spoke them out loud.

"If we stay, we die. If we run, they will hunt us down.

Let's not fool ourselves. The Silver Kingdom is going down, but this shouldn't happen till the last one of us goes down. I say we fight. I say we make it the night where old men, women and children fought. I say we lay down our candles and pick up our swords."

"Well said, young fella," said the silver soldier. "But even if you all gathered your courage to fight. There are no more swords nor spears for all of you. Our weapons are laying down in the hands of our dead soldiers downhill!" he added, but the Mute signalled back, "I know where to get our weapons. The weapons that are waiting for us at the shore, the weapons the Merchant put there, are the ones we will hold in our hands. We will climb down to the beach from around the hill to get there faster, and our mothers will stay here, and they will beat the war drums for every pirate and red soldier to hear."

Chapter 77

"The pirates almost wiped out the Silver fleet. Only a few of the Merchant's men were still alive and fighting. The Saharan took out one defence wave after another while making his way uphill, getting closer and closer to the Sliver Arched Towers. Only a few tired silver soldiers were left. They could not beat the Saharan or defend and hold the shore. Sooner or later, the pirates and the red soldiers would swarm in the Silver Kingdom."

All those thoughts ran through the mind of The Silver King as he saw the last bunch of the Silver Guards lining up for battle. He paused and waited.

He didn't send the soldiers downhill right away to wave another attack against the Saharan and his men.

He was reluctant, for this was not just another wave of attack. It was the last one by the very last line of silver soldiers.

"My King," said one of the silver soldiers.

"What is it now?" the Silver King answered.

"The villagers, they want to fight. They bought their swords and want to fight," said the silver soldier.

"What? But we don't have any more armour for them!" the Silver King stated.

"They know, my King, they know!" the Silver Soldier said.

The Silver King looked behind the soldier and saw the

silver people and the Mute holding the Merchant's blue swords and spears in their hands. The Mute stepped up to him. The Mute stood on a rock, and as hard as he could, he stuck the sword right into the middle of the rock so that both of his hands would be free to sign his words.

"We know you have no armour," he signalled, and his twin brother spoke it out loud. "But we also know that the armour won't stop the Reds from stabbing our hearts. The only way to stop them is to fight them, and we want to fight with you."

The Silver King seemed annoyed by the Mute's words, so he gently pushed the Mute back from the sword in the rock and said to them all.

"Go! Run away. There is no place for you in battle. It is our doom. Run all of you. Such a battle can't be won by a bunch of old men, women, and children."

The Silver King tried to pull the Mute's sword out of the rock, but it seemed to be stuck, he kept on trying, but the sword didn't loosen up. He pulled harder, yet still, the sword stayed in the rock. Here the Mute jumped back on the rock and then signalled as his twin said his words,

"Yes, we might die. Some of us might die if we fight, but if we don't, all of us will. We march with you bravely because we also know that it is not the weapons in our hands nor the armour on our chests that our enemy fears, but it's what's in our hearts...for brave hearts kill far more enemies than sharp swords and when they will see our bare hearts they will know that our hearts are brave and yes. Yes, we are a bunch of old men, women, and children in your eyes, and yes, we don't have any armour, we don't have any horses, but you know that we, we are your last legion, and we, we are walking to battle."

The Mute finished his speech and grabbed his sword, pulling it out of the rock while everyone yelled for battle.

Chapter 78

Three lines of red soldiers on the Teardrop Isle kept their eyes on the bushes and trees, ready to fight the Merchant, while their leader kept his eyes on the Red Castle's shore, waiting for a signal to start a double attack and come in on the Merchant from both ends; and then he saw it, the attack flag was waved.

"March up," he commanded his men, and they moved into the isle carefully. However, at the exact moment, the Saharan signalled all on-shore forces to the borderline, as he saw a large number of Silvers lining uphill to attack.

The three lines of red soldiers who went in didn't know where the Merchant was, but it was worse knowing they were now going in on their own.

They were almost sure they would not defeat the Merchant, for all the soldiers who were sent after him never returned. They heard them scream, cry, and plead, but they never returned. Nonetheless, they stepped in while pirates and red soldiers aboard Venus kept their eyes on the Isle and closely watched them as they disappeared behind the isle's deep trees and bushes.

Chapter 79

The painter's hands were shaking as he tried hard to hold them steady and finish painting the Red King, who placed his throne over the rubbles and sat quietly.

It was tough to ignore the sounds of the battles going around. The ships' cannons and the Royal Guards' swords clung closer and closer to the throne Hall.

The Red King didn't move. He was abnormally still and gloomy. He looked like he cared for nothing, worried about nothing. As if he was in a dark…dark side of some sort of meditation.

The painter dropped the brush out of fear as he turned and saw the First Man standing at the door. None of the Royal Guards could stop him. All of them were killed.

The First Man stood at the door, holding his dangling sword in one hand and Prima's ring in the other.

The Painter dropped his jaw in fear for his own life, but the First Man said,

"I am not here for you!" instantly, the painter ran, stumbled, and sprinted out of the throne hall as he passed the First Man in a blink.

"Can you feel it?" said the Red King while still gazing in his darkness.

"It is dark," he added. "Love lightens you up, but the loss of it darkens you. It is dark and cold. It either gets the best out of you or the worst. My anger is now subtle but mighty. You must be feeling the same, aren't you?" asked the Red King.

"You killed her! You ordered your Slayers to kill her! She was too beautiful to be killed!" said the First Man with dripping tears and anger.

"Yes," sighed the Red King, "You are riding the same darkness as I am." The Red King stood up, drew his sword, and opened his arms.

"Come. Let the might of our darkness meet on the edges of blades."

The First Man ran at the Red King, wielded his sword with all the anger he had inside him, and their swords crossed, clanged, and sparked.

Chapter 80

Pirates and Red soldiers aboard Venus kept their eyes on the isle's tree line, waiting for the red soldiers to come out, hoping they had captured the Merchant and killed the Beast.

Trees shook, and screams rumbled. Then a long moment of silence followed before the Merchant leapt out of the isle on the Beast's back with Isabella holding on to him.

They leapt into the waters, and quickly the Beast tossed the Merchant and Isabella off his back towards the bowline. Isabella screamed as she held on tighter to the Merchant, who quickly grabbed the bowline and climbed up to the figurehead.

Pirate ships fired at the Beast, and the Red soldiers threw their spears at it, but the Beast wasn't easy to beat. It wouldn't fall quickly, giving the Merchant some time to act, to reach the leveller, unleash the cannons, and free his men.

Isabella held on to Venus' figurehead, and the Merchant stepped quickly onto the main deck. He fought one pirate after another, one red soldier after another, trying to reach the leveller, but they were too many, one move after another, one wound after another; the Merchant was tiring out and yet still couldn't reach the leveller.

One skilled pirate managed to sneak behind the Merchant, turn quickly to cross swords with the Merchant and suddenly stabbed him from the side with a dagger.

Isabella screamed and cried as the Merchant fell to his knees, covered in blood from his wounds.

The pirates rounded up and pointed their swords at the Merchant's throat,

"The key," a pirate demanded.

The Merchant looked at his shirt. It all turned red; he was bleeding from too many wounds. He spat some blood and breathed rapidly, looked back at the Beast being taken down by fire and spears, and looked at Isabella as she desperately held on to the figurehead's pole.

"All right," said the Merchant, hardly lifting himself. Then he walked toward the figurehead.

The pirates and the red soldiers waited with their swords in their hands as they couldn't all follow the Merchant on the narrow back of the figurehead.

Back in the Red Castle, the Red King and the First Man fought fiercely.

The Red King was stronger than the First Man thought; one attack after another ended with the First Man thrown to the floor on his back.

The Silvers uphill raised their flags for one last battle with the Saharan and his men.

The pirates' cannons shattered the last silver ship.

And the Black Family's Dean uphill popped a bottle of champagne.

The Merchant passed Isabella and reached the far tip of the pole. He dropped down heavily and just laid there.

Everyone, including Isabella, didn't quite understand what the Merchant was doing, but they all assumed that he was getting the key or that he had just dropped dead or unconscious.

The Merchant then stretched his arms and reached Venus' face; he wrapped his palms around it and pressed its eyes with his fingers. Instantly Venus' mouth clicked open, and a couple of small gold daggers popped out. The Merchant held one in each hand, stood up and pressed his feet on the figurehead's back, two golden spiked soles locked on his boots, and he stretched his arms open with both golden daggers in his hands. He seemed so focused and quiet. Suddenly, the sea waters seemed so quiet and calm. No one knew what was going on, and the fear of the unknown crawled into their hearts.

Slowly, a set of small waves started to form around the ships. Each wave made its way towards Venus; Then, all the waves merged into one big unturned wave and moved quicker and quicker towards Venus' bow, gaining more speed and more and more size as it got closer. Everyone looked at the wave in fear because it didn't form from where it should, not from the horizon, not to Venus' star side. It formed sideways to shore. The wave mounted up just under Venus' figurehead. It lifted the bow so high and plunged the stern so low that everyone held onto something so as not to fall off the back into the waters.

The pirates and the red soldiers hung to the ropes as they gazed in awe at the Merchant standing over Venus' figurehead, rising above them all.

Isabella held on tight to the pole, and while everyone lost balance, the Merchant stood still, with his feet pinned by the spiked soles to the back of Venus' figurehead that was now opening its mouth and its eyes dripping tears of blood, the Merchant's blood that covered his hands.

Thunder roared in the skies, rain fell, and the wind blew. As the wave continued to the Stern, the bow dropped, and the Merchant front flipped and leapt in the air over the Pirates' heads and landed right behind them as they slid to the figurehead.

The Silvers with the Mute beside the Silver King ran downhill, yelling for battle and holding their swords high while the mothers beat the war drums.

The First Man struggled more and more and couldn't beat the Red King, not even scratch him with his sword.

After the Merchant landed behind the pirates and the red soldiers, they were all off balance and couldn't fight him. With his gold daggers, the Merchant slit them all to death one after another, they were screaming in fear and pain until the deck was clear, and the Merchant reached the leveller and pulled it.

Down on the fire floor, PaleFace saw the hatches open; he shouted out, "Load" They all loaded the cannons with gunpowder, "Switch range," commanded PaleFace.

At the same time, the Silvers stormed down on the Saharan lines with great force. The lines slammed into each other; many fell. The Silver King spotted the Saharan in battle and ran to him to confront him, but the Saharan was quicker, and he stabbed the Silver King in the neck.

Taking advantage of the Saharan's distraction, the Mute jumped over his shoulders and stabbed the Saharan to death. The Silvers flamed up and fought with all their strength.

More Pirates and Red soldiers climbed aboard Venus to fight the Merchant, but he took them down one after the other as the giant wave washed the pirate ships away from Venus.

As soon as the cannons were in place, PaleFace shouted, "Fire."

Venus' long-range cannons bombarded the Red Castle and the Red soldiers ashore.

"Retreat"

The Silvers ran back uphill, leaving Venus to finish the battle. The short-range cannons fired down the pirate ships shattering them to the seabed, while the Merchant took out everyone on the main deck.

All the cannons fired at once, and the Dean overlooking his loss broke his champagne flute as he clinched on it in anger.

As the cannon balls hit the walls of the Red Castle, the First Man, desperately trying to kill the Red King, used the opportunity, threw his sword, and leapt towards the Red King, holding him firmly and jumping into the line of fire, ending both of their lives.

PaleFace fired, switched ranges, and cued the cannons

like a master gunner. A symphony he played. A symphony with Venus' guns that fired for the rest of the night, flattening the Red Castle to the ground.

It was almost dawn when the cannons stopped firing. The mist and the smoke screened Venus from sight.

The remaining red soldiers on shore searched for survivors between the rubble. They saw a woman's hand, covered in blood and tar, shaking and waving from underneath the rubble. It was all dusty and bloody; they quickly dug out the woman and were overwhelmed as it turned out to be the Queen herself.

The Queen looked around in shock at the battle's aftermaths. It was worse than anything she thought she would ever see. The Red Castle was destroyed, bodies of the dead laying all around, limbs scattered, and blood running in streams to ponds of clotted blood. The Red soldiers helped take her hand to help her walk a few steps towards the shore, where she saw the worst site. She looked up to the horizon, to the sea. As the smoke and mist cleared out, Venus was gone; all the Merchant's ships vanished with only a few traces of debris floating over the waters. No one saw him sail away, and no one surely knows if he ever did.

With slow, trembling steps, the Queen leaned on the Red Guards to reach the hill's top, where she looked for the Merchant, but still, the horizon was clear. There was no sign of the Merchant's fleet nor the battle.

The waters were clear. And no one has ever seen the Merchant or his fleet ever since.

Chapter 81

"What happened?" asked the sailor. Now the storm is slamming waves up the lighthouse "some say that the Merchant took out all the pirates and sailed away so swiftly that no one saw him. Some say he escaped and hid with his love Isabella on some island away from the world. Some believe that he sailed up to the skies or down to the deep. No one knows where the Merchant and his fleet went, but everyone knows, for sure, that whoever has seen, met, or heard about the Merchant will never forget him nor will forget the magnificence of his fleet," answered the old Keeper.

"What about the rest? What happened to the rest?" asked the sailor as thunderstruck in the skies.

"The Mute became the new and youngest ever Silver King after the Silvers were almost wiped out in the battle, and he married his girl and made peace with the Reds. As for the Blacks, the Dean ran, and they returned to their shadows," said the old Keeper as the winds whistled through the lighthouse.

"And the Queen. What happened to the Queen?"

The old Keeper turned and looked out of the window, deep into the horizon and spoke his words out of even deeper thought,

"The Queen?"

"Yes. The Queen," said the sailor.

"The Queen stood there all day long. From dawn till dusk, she searched the horizon for any sign of the Merchant. And when the night fell, she commanded her guards to bring her a torch. She held it up high all night for the Merchant to find his way back to shore if he was up there in the seas trying to return. Or at least she might soften his heart into showing up again if he saw her torch lit all night.

The longer the Merchant was gone, the wider hardship spread. Poverty, illnesses, and starvation shaded the lands. The darker it got, the more guilty the Queen felt. The more guilty she felt, the longer she stood on that hill holding the light for the Merchant to return.

She held the torch till her arms and feet shook and went numb.

Day after day, night after night, month after month, and year after year.

Eventually, she grew too old to hold the torch all night. They built her a statue, a copper statue that would stand atop the hill, lighting the torch every single night. She grew old, and she grew sick. She gathered her knights and made them pledge to her that they would keep the torch lit every night. They pledged to reach every shore, every bay and every port and light a torch all night. She passed away, but her knights kept their promise. All over the world, over ice, grass and sand, they kept the torch alit over mountains, hills, and Islands. We… rode horses, sailed ships, climbed rocks and kept our pledge; we kept the light. People started to call us the light keepers, and when we started to build ourselves houses, they called us the lighthouse keepers. Yes, the lighthouse keepers.

"You! You are one of them? You are a knight!" said the sailor in awe as the storm outside roared louder and louder.

Just before night fell, the sailor stepped out of the lighthouse while the storm was still at large.

"Are you waiting for him?" the sailor recalled asking the old Keeper as he stopped walking and looked up to the lighthouse. He saw the shadow of the old Keeper standing next to the glass window and remembered his words.

"Him, or anyone like him. Anyone who stands for what he stood for might be him, who fights for what he fought for, who defends what he believed, could be him, anyone who serves the good he served...is him."

The old Keeper pulled a leveller, a chain rattled, and the large lamp lit up bright. The sailor heard the Queen in his head commanding out loud, "Light it up," and he saw it. He saw the light beaming up from one place on the horizon to the other. It rained heavily. He put his hand in his bag and felt a book inside that didn't belong to him. He pulled it out, and there it was, a book that belonged to the Merchant. He looked up the lighthouse once more and saw the old Keeper's shadow standing next to the lamp, but as the lightning flashed, the old Keeper was gone. Yet still, his words echoed in the sailor's head.

"And now you've heard my story, judge it. Judge every person, every intention, and every action. Judge it, for one's judgment, reveals nothing but oneself. What would you have done? Whom would you have helped? Whom would you have stopped? Judge it, for out there, on those lands, there will always be a Red King, there will always be the Queen, there will always be the Blacks, the pirate, and the brave Mute, but there won't always be the Merchant. As for us, the light-keepers, we wait. We keep the light throughout the night. We don't watch the world burn. We turn and keep the light for the good one to return."

The sailor turned to the sea and saw the light of a ship close to shore.

He raised his hand while holding the book tightly as he recalled the old Keeper's last words to him,

"And now...and before you take another step, choose... choose a home...or a ship."

The End

Inspirations

YouTube:

General theme + end battle
https://youtu.be/7QU1nvuxaMA

She the Queen
https://youtu.be/RYPWxymohWs

Royal Anger
https://youtu.be/yVIRcnlRKF8

The Knights' Pledge
https://youtu.be/aAsqalYR_dU

Escaping the Red Castle
https://youtu.be/ZagsLrNzg3I

The fleet's war drums
https://youtu.be/GC-JjWSYwhU

The Queen's emotional agony
https://youtu.be/5yP9olT_TdM

Sound Cloud:

The Keeper and the sailor - from beginning to end
https://soundcloud.app.goo.gl/ize4Ub49XSNqFdV17

Summoning the Blacks
https://soundcloud.app.goo.gl/Y1qDyLpaM6d8wFJd9

Dawn of war

https://soundcloud.app.goo.gl/W2TqZyr3nxHjSmta6

She moved to music better than a silk curtain to a summer breeze.

https://soundcloud.app.goo.gl/sNySewtWvRKMERqX6

The first man - the blade must have been cold & dropping the coins.

https://soundcloud.app.goo.gl/RC8T3bhtkUE6CcbQ8

Last of the Silvers - walking to battle.
https://soundcloud.app.goo.gl/H1g3xL2C61XTwLKL9

The Merchant whispers to Isabella
https://soundcloud.app.goo.gl/1LGfWYsCkNNoo2K3A

The Merchant - Jai Kai - the rope
https://soundcloud.app.goo.gl/SSzauV4GXYwrXYTM7

iTunes

Prima wondered at night.

https://music.apple.com/eg/album/mad-about-you-orchestra-version/503867148?i=503867224

Stories & Legacies

Zheng Hu

Santa Isabella

Arthur

Cinderella

Hunchback of Notre Dame

Red Riding Hood

Structures

Statue of Liberty

Lighthouses

Coffee

Seven Fortunes

Edited By
Judy Lambert
lambjk@hotmail.com

Cover Painted by
Diala Naguib
Instagram @dialanaguib

Contact Author

www.sherifelhotabiy.com

Email: info@sherifelhotabiy.com
Instagram: @sherif_hotabiy
Tiktok: @sherifelhotabiy
Twitter: @sherifelhotabiy

Facebook page: Sherif EL-Hotabiy

#The_Merchant_the_Novel

CPSIA information can be obtained
at www.ICGtesting.com
Printed in the USA
LVHW111941271022
731593LV00007B/129